A
Handbook
for
Drowning

A Handbook for Drowning

Stories

by

David Shields

Alfred A. Knopf

New York

1991

THIS IS A BORZOI BOOK
PUBLISHED BY ALFRED A. KNOPF, INC.

Portions of this book were originally published, sometimes under
different titles and in substantially different form, in the following
publications: "The Sixties" in *Harper's*; "Father's Day" in *The Village Voice*;
"Ode to the Donner Party" in *Story*; "War Wounds" in *Conjunctions*; "The
Imaginary Dead Baby Sea Gull" in *Between C and D*; "The Heroic Mode"
in *Agni*; "The Gun in the Grass at Your Feet" in *The Quarterly*; "The War
on Poverty" in *Four Quarters*; "Heart of a Dybbuk" in *Confrontation*; "The
Moon, Falling" in *Black River Review*; "Contemporary Film Criticism" in
Movieworks; "Lies," "Junk," and "Oaxaca" in *Lake Effect*; "Northern Light"
in *On the Edge*; and "Babies" in *Northern Light*.

Two sections of "War Wounds" appeared in "Mother's Child" in *Vital
Lines: Contemporary Fiction About Medicine* (St. Martin's Press). One
section of "A Brief Survey of Ideal Desire" is adapted from "A Note on the
Conclusion of 'The Dead,' " which appeared in *The James Joyce Quarterly*;
another section of "A Brief Survey of Ideal Desire" is adapted from "The
War on Poverty," which appeared in *Four Quarters*. One section of "Lies"
appeared as "Nothing" in *Sun Dog: The Southeast Review*.

The author would like to thank these magazines and St. Martin's Press
for permission to reprint, the University of Washington Graduate School
and St. Lawrence University for their support, and most especially Peter
Bailey for his invaluable criticism of repeated drafts of the manuscript.

Library of Congress Cataloging-in-Publication Data
Shields, David.
A handbook for drowning / David Shields.—1st ed.
p.   cm.
ISBN 0-679-40111-3
I. Title.
PS3569.H4834H36   1991
813' .54—dc20   90-28456   CIP

Manufactured in the United States of America
First Edition

FOR MY FATHER

Contents

The Imaginary Dead Baby Sea Gull   3

Gookus Explains the Eternal Mysteries   13

The War on Poverty   19

The Heroic Mode   29

The Gun in the Grass at Your Feet   35

A Brief Survey of Ideal Desire   39

Sudden Affection   47

Northern Light   53

Lies   55

The Moon, Falling   63

The Sixties   73

The Sheer Joy of Amoral Creation   79

Father's Day   87

Junk   93

Oaxaca   103

The Fourth Wonder of the World   109

Heart of a Dybbuk   119

Comp Lit 101: Walt Grows Up   127

Contemporary Film Criticism   135

Ode to the Donner Party   137

Babies   143

Interference   147

War Wounds   155

Innocence   173

Imagine yourself a strong swimmer.
— SUSAN LUDVIGSON, *The Swimmer*

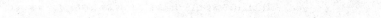

A
Handbook
for
Drowning

The Imaginary Dead Baby Sea Gull

"Scratch me," Nina said, so I scratched, like an alley cat I scratched. She turned over, lay face down in the sand, and untied the back of her swimsuit top. She folded her arms into a cradle and rested her head, shut her eyes. I was sitting on top of her and she was stretched out in front of me. With my ragged nails I scratched until the muscles in the tips of my fingers ached, until her skin became red and splotched and free of itches. I would have scratched until I had stripped away all of her skin, peeled off layers of dermis and epidermis and sebaceous glands, picked away at the backbone and spine, I would have played around with the vertebrae had not Nina said, "Softer, you're hurting me."

I lay down next to her in the clammy sand and softly

kneaded her, stroked her back, and rubbed the tension out of her rigid neck muscles and shoulder blades. With the edge of my fingernail I drew lines straight as razors, sharp as knives down her side. I scratched her scalp. I planted salty wet kisses in the middle of her spine. I massaged her horizontally, vertically, diagonally. Her ear was a conch and my voice was the Pacific Ocean, my tongue was the waves, and I whispered into her ear and told her the secrets of the sea. But Nina didn't answer. She didn't respond. She felt good all over and breathed little sighs of exhaustion and began to sleep.

It was dawn. Nina was asleep and oblivious of the clear crystal morning and uninterested, simply not interested, she would have said if she were awake, because she'd established a sleep cycle as an important aspect of her life, which I'd rudely disrupted the night before and which she was now in the process of restoring. She liked to dream and explain the unconscious to me when she awoke, but now it was morning. She was asleep and I was awake, watching the morning rise.

I cupped sand in my palms and sprinkled thin streams of granules up and down her back as if from an hourglass. I was Time and her back was tabula rasa, but nothing happened: she didn't budge. She dozed and dreamed and corrected her sleep cycle. I blew hot breath into the pores of her skin, gathered her hair—covered her back nearly to her waist with her locks—and got under her swimsuit bottom by grabbing the folds of her gooseflesh, but Nina was nothing if not a sound sleeper. Once her eyes were shut she was dead to the world, and so she napped.

We were alone on this dismal beach; there wasn't a soul in sight, only Nina, and she was snoring and wanted no part of me for the moment. I took a comb from her canvas bag and drew pictures in the sand. I erased the sketches, leveling the area, then lifted my white polo shirt over my head and spread it on the flush surface of the sand in front of me.

"Nina," I whispered, but she continued to daydream. I emptied the contents of her bag onto my shirt. "Nina," I said once more and made sure she was still asleep, which she was. I ransacked her stuff, her hairbrush with a handle made of cracked green glass and tufts of knotted hair wrapped around the bristles and her black comb wedged into the middle of the brush; pins of all sorts, broken bobby pins and safety pins and hairpins; enough Kleenex in every color of the rainbow to kill her ceaseless colds; her fountain pen; her white diaphragm case. I jingled her keys, none of which opened doors or locks easily anymore because Nina had so badly mangled them in various fits of anger, and I counted her change, mostly pennies.

I wanted to know more. I wanted to know everything. I opened her wallet. I shuffled through the cards in the pockets and plastic flaps: discount cards to theaters that no longer existed, calendars of holidays she didn't know and didn't care to know and never celebrated, her expired driver's license, her library card on which her name was misspelled. And no color snapshots of herself or her friends or former lovers, only black-and-white photographs of my face, scowling into infinity, ugly as sin. I flipped through the pages of her date book (of weekly appointments with her shrink and the number of hours she slept each night) and the pages of her red address book (the addresses and telephone numbers of people whom she considered special but who really had very little use for her). And I read her lists—endless, unhappy catalogues of things she should do and chores to occupy her time, which, when done, were blackened until unreadable, scratched out with a felt-tip pen until the entire page of duties was slightly indented, at which point she'd conjured up a new list of things to do.

Sea gulls were walking on the shore as if they owned it and I shooed them away, told them to scat. They did: they spread their pearl-gray wings and soared up into the air toward those hulking sand dunes down at the other end of the beach and off the shore a ways. I turned my eyes from the sun, which was brighter now and blazing equidistant between the sea and the top of the sky. Waves came surging from somewhere out in the middle of the ocean, pushed the shoreline back, and deposited algae and splintered driftwood on the beach.

"Nina," I said. Still sound asleep. I knelt down in the sand, picked up her journal, held it in my hands, and riffled through its pages—thin, translucent sheets of white onionskin that were unnumbered, unlettered, and tied together at the top and bottom and to the back cover in a tight knot with twine. The front and back covers were made of thick cardboard. The front was painted white and had her name printed in Gothic letters in greasepaint in the top right-hand corner, and the back was chrome yellow. She wrote in splotched ink from a fountain pen. The ink had a pure, diluted quality to it, a kind of grainy black that intimated unequivocal truth, and her handwriting, uniform and flowing, promised more of the same: closed-off loops and swirls occurred at exactly the right moments, crossed *t*'s flew across the page, and actual periods rather than dashes ended sentences. Nina was under the impression that everything mine was hers, everything hers was mine, and I folded back the cardboard front cover of her journal. Nina thought no act, even murder, she said, could be malicious in her eyes, if I had committed it. She loved me that much, and I focused my eyes on the first word of the first sentence on the first page of her journal.

His Body. We were walking down an alley late at night. There were only dark houses and bushes on either side of us and the promise of dogs. I admit it—I was scared—and Walter, poor Walter, must pretend he's never scared. I wanted him to take my hand or hold my shoulder or do something nice and reassuring like whistle, but instead he tripped over a fallen tree twig and landed on the gravel, quite bruised and horribly embarrassed. His hands were cut. His hands are like claws. He squeezes so hard and I tell him to stop, but he squeezes harder and says he's letting me know he's still there. He's always still right there, pawing away at me. He invited me to a movie and we sat way in back. I can't see the screen very well that far away, but Walter insisted we sit in the last row. It was quite dark and the cushions were ripped out of the seats, so we were practically sitting on steel springs. He kept knocking knees with me, and I kept sliding over on the torn seat until I was leaning halfway into the aisle. In the movie, bodies were falling here and there, colliding, going through contortions of all kinds. Extremely attractive male and female bodies were unclothed and in color. I wanted to watch the movie—I'd never imagined half the positions—but Walter was knocking his knobby left knee against my thigh and his right leg was draped over the broken back of the chair in front of him and he was laughing. Laughing at lust! Poor Walter.

I thought about the movie and laughed again, causing Nina to stir. I closed the journal, put it back in her beach bag along with the rest of her things. Laying the bag down where it had been, right near her, next to her feet, I tickled her toes, especially the middle toe of her left foot, stubby, deformed, bereft of toenail, and without any real sensation since very early one morning when she was seven years old and stepped right on a rusted nail while trying to pick up speed in a homemade go-cart called *El Fuego*. In order to save her whole foot from being amputated, half the toe was severed. I tickled what was left of it and moved on to her other toes, her big toes and her pinkies and the scrunched-up arches of nail and flesh in between.

"What were you laughing about?" she asked.

"A baby sea gull nose-dived into the water. It wings just stopped flapping."

"The poor thing. Is it all right?" she asked.

"No," I said. "It drowned. It didn't know how to swim."

"Why didn't you save it?" she asked.

"It was halfway out at sea. I would have saved it if I could."

She cried.

"Don't cry," I said.

With my fingernails I picked away at the calluses on her heel until the hard, thickened skin gave way. I peeled it off and rubbed the tan backs of her legs, the tough muscles and tendons and the bony crevices behind her knees. I moved up her body toward the back of her thighs and hams and explored the area around her loins, but when I so much as touched her back she squealed and slapped my hand away.

"My back's on fire," Nina said.

I tied and knotted the back of her swimsuit top and hitched her swimsuit bottom up higher on her hips. Nina turned around and brushed the sand out of her face and the sleep out of her eyes. She sat up and caught her first glimpse of the sun. It was high noon, and the sun, directly over us, glanced down and off the surface of the sea. We walked to the water's edge, stood in mud and slosh, then walked farther into the ocean. Waves splashed about our lower legs. I let go of her hand and belly-flopped into the sea. I did the Australian crawl, the breaststroke, the butterfly. I did the sidestroke. I floated on my back. I treaded water. I swam out to where the imaginary dead baby sea gull would have drowned, and I swam back underwater and snapped up Nina's legs.

"No, don't," she said as she splashed into the Pacific and I dragged her out toward deeper water. "I don't like to swim." Nina blew bubbles, slapped at the surf with her hands, turned her body this way and that, paddled her feet occasionally. She swam fine. I flipped her onto her back and told her to float.

"Walter, I told you, I don't—"

"Everybody likes to float," I said.

She puffed out her breasts and made rotating circles in the water with her arms, even called upon a frog kick to propel herself slowly away from shore. "The water's not bad at all," she said. "This is fun." She was a natural floater and she shut her eyes, sang pop melodies almost in key, let herself drift.

I called from the shore, "Looking good," but she didn't hear me—she was already nearly rounding the corner of our little cove—so I hurriedly dried myself off with a towel, sank down in the sand, and opened up her beach bag again to read her journal.

BYOG. Walter takes me to the strangest places. We went to a run-down bar with a door you could hardly open, splintered and without a handle. No one was dancing, least of all us, because I don't dance in public. My body's a private thing; it doesn't belong to the world at large. It was such a cheap place you actually had to bring your own glasses, and Walter pulled a couple of dirty glasses out of his coat pocket. "Let's go, Walter, let's go somewhere else that's quieter," I said, but he put the glasses on the counter and ordered a double bourbon for himself, asking me what I wanted until I finally said, "The same," because he was getting impatient and I couldn't decide. We sat at a caved-in table in the back of the bar. Walter got up every so often to get himself more liquor. I have never seen anyone drink so much so fast in my life. Everyone in the bar was shouting their lungs out and the band was playing so loud that I couldn't hear Walter, who was carrying on about some aspect of the music. I kept drinking whiskeys right along with him in order to stay sane. Walter leaned over and asked if I wanted to dance and I said, "No, Walter, not here," and he stood up and tugged on my arm and I said, "Goddamnit, not now, not here." The jazz was loud and noisy and shitty and the drummer had only one arm. On his left side was just a sleeve that flapped against his shoulder. Interestingly, he was better than anyone else in the band. We were the only ones dancing and Walter did the mambo wildly and spun into the wall and collapsed, poor Walter. . . . We stumbled up the hill to my apartment.

Nina pounded her arms and paddled her legs, floating ashore. She stood up when her feet hit bottom, took the towel from around my neck, and dried herself off as we walked back up the beach to our hideaway. Nina was determined to restore her sleep cycle by the end of the day, so she sat up against the rocks with the towel rolled up behind her head, her feet crossed, and her arms folded under her white swimsuit top, and slept some more.

The tide was higher than it had been all day and rising. There wasn't much shore left for the gulls to prowl, so they were out at sea, perched on rocks or skimming the surface of the ocean, hunting for late-afternoon snacks. It was colder, too. A light wind was coming in off the water. I shook Nina awake. She changed into her jeans and picked up her backpack, and I picked up mine. I carried our sleeping bags, walking ahead of her along the backshore toward the sand dunes. I wanted a final view of the Pacific from the top of the dunes.

We couldn't leave the same way we came—the tide blocked off access to the path through the cliff in back of us—and we were able to get off the beach and onto land only by crossing a river which once had fed the ocean but which was dry now and the source only of gutted rowboats, then scrambling up a spiral staircase, which emptied out onto the pier overlooking the beach. Nina had her troubles; she nearly lost her balance standing up in one of those damn rowboats, and she all but lost her breath for good climbing the rickety steps. I took her backpack for her and so I was weighted down—two sleeping bags and both our backpacks and shoes filled with sand.

Nina was tired and hungry. She wanted to leave behind the beach, the sand, the dunes altogether, but I dragged her along through the dry grass and the weeds toward the hills. I ran toward a sand dune that was high enough to provide a good view, and steep, but not too steep to climb. Nina preferred to stay down at the bottom and rest. "You can tell me about it," she said, but I shoved her up the slope. It took us awhile, but we made it to the top. She would lose her footing and fall to her knees in the sand, sliding down-hill until I could grasp her by the arm or leg and boost her back up.

"Lie down," I whispered for some reason. "I'll make you a bed."

I would have built up the sand around her and covered her body, heaped sand upon her from top to bottom and pinned her shoulders had not Nina said, "No, I'm not tired." She'd straightened out her sleep cycle. She faced the sea, watched the sun sit on the water out at the horizon and the full tide flood the empty beach and chip away at rock near us, right below the dunes, and then she sat down and took the fountain pen and journal out of her bag, removed the top from the pen, turned her journal to an empty page in the middle of the book, and wrote, then handed it to me when she was finished.

The Sea Gull. Walter, will you please take a quick swim out to sea to check if the sea gull is still alive? Maybe it is— maybe it made it onto a rock out there and didn't drown. I don't want to feel responsible for its death. I don't want to leave the beach with a guilty conscience. Please, Walter, please check. If it did drown, shouldn't we bury it or at least report it to someone in charge of the beach, the game warden or whoever? What I don't understand is how you could have simply watched it drown. Why didn't you try to save it? I would have, and I don't swim half as well as you do. I just don't think I understand you, Walter. When will you stop laughing at misery? I'm so sick and tired of your pseudo-strength. All I want you to do is laugh at what is funny and cry at what isn't, but you won't do that, will you? Please, Walter, see if it's still alive.

I held her fountain pen in my hand and thought about leaving Nina stranded on top of the sand dune, diving headfirst into high tide, and swimming against the current to see if the bird was still alive; plunging down to the bottom of the ocean and scrounging around for a dead sea gull; telling Nina that the baby sea gull had no chance of survival because it had never existed, that I'd read the first two entries in her journal and would make it my business to skip the rest—all these things I thought about and shook my head. I lifted the metal tip of the pen off the page and gave her capped pen, her closed journal back to her.

Gookus Explains the Eternal Mysteries

Although he was fat and exceedingly ugly and the same age as I was (eleven), the Gookus knew more about it than I did, much more, so I sat on my bed with my back to the wooden wall and my feet dangling over the side of the bed, and listened as Gary—my great Gookus with his Buddha stomach—told me absolutely everything he knew about the subject, waddling around the room, sucking on cigarettes, stuffing dirty clothes into the crack of the door, turning on the overhead light when it got dark in my basement bedroom, the heater when it got cold, the radio when he grew weary of hearing his own high voice. For hours in an empty parking lot, which had just been black-topped and painted and was still wet, he had kissed Yvonne Rasnick until she cried and shuddered and Gookus did not know what to do, so he stopped. He had felt up Teri Schraeder, who, whatever else one might want to say about her, was not flat. He had already started masturbating; on bad nights he rubbed raw skin sores until he bled, but on good nights he came. Sort of. He opened his wallet and showed me his rubber. He tried to explain to me a lot of highly Latinate terminology. He had found stacks and stacks of *Playboys* behind the books in the cabinets of his father's study, and when his father was away, Gookus would go in and not leave until he had been transfixed by a picture to urge him through the night. He had seen his mother, walking from the shower to the bedroom, naked.

"What did she look like?" I asked.

"She looked like my mother."

"But naked, I mean."

"Good. Real good."

"Like the women in the magazines?"

"No. Wetter. Older. Fatter. Hairier. But still good, Walt."

"How do you kiss?"

"I used to kiss my mother quickly on the cheek before I went to bed."

"And now?"

"I don't."

"But I mean real kissing. How do you kiss girls?"

"On the lips."

"What do you do?"

"You tilt your head."

"To which side?"

"The left," Gookus explained. "You tilt your head, you close your eyes, then you put your lips on her lips. You open your mouth and make long, wet kisses. You close your mouth and make short, dry, little ones. You put your tongue in her mouth."

"Your tongue? Doesn't she choke?"

"No. She moans."

"Where do your hands go, Gookus, and your legs and the rest of your body? What do you do with yourself?"

"You put your hands in her hair and your legs go behind you."

"I can't imagine it. I can't see it."

"I'll show you."

"What do I do with my nose, Gookus? Won't it bop her in the face?"

"Let me show you."

"What do I do with my stomach—suck it in so she doesn't feel it or puff it out so it rubs against her? I need to know these things. I'm afraid I'll forget."

"Let me show you."

"No."

"Yes."

"Leave me alone," I said.

Gookus put down his cigarette, turned up the volume a little on the radio for background music, and sat down next to me on the bed. Before I knew what was happening, he had pushed me down and was rolling on top of me, sliding up and down my legs, and laughing. He was laughing. He pressed his thick, rough lips to mine, kissed me on the cheeks, the pimpled nose, the chin. Gookus blew hot air and whispered obscene nothings into my ear. I learned fast: we French-kissed. But the first kiss of my life didn't last for long because when he started fooling around with my zipper I sat up, pushed him off me, and rolled away. I tried to hit him in the face, but he caught my fist, twisted my right arm, and shoved me off the bed onto the floor. He pounced on me. All ninety-five pounds of him landed with full force and then he sat on me, bouncing up and down on my chest while he pinned my arms and legs.

"Give," he said.

He pinched my skin.

"Give," he said.

He Indian-rubbed my wrist.

"Give," he said.

He kneed me in the groin.

I gave.

Gookus got off and let me up, and I hurried away from him into the bathroom. I looked at my flushed face in the mirror, then dunked my head in a basin full of cold water and dried myself with a towel. Gookus barged into the bathroom to take a piss, flushing before he was through, wiping his hands on his pants—what a Neanderthal. Out of nowhere and down the windowpane crawled a black spider. It wasn't a symbol of this or that; it was just a spider. Gookus tried to smash the poor little unpoisonous thing with my favorite bathroom book, Maury Wills's autobiography, but he missed and the spider continued to crawl toward the floor. Before he was able to try again, I grabbed his arm and said, "Don't. Don't, Gookus. Don't kill it. Leave it alone."

"Why?"

"Just leave it alone. It's not hurting anything."

Gookus picked up Maury Wills's autobiography again.

I cupped the spider in my hands, placed it on the windowsill, opened the window, and flicked the spider into the garden.

"Why did you do that, Walt? I wanted to kill it."

"Well, I didn't want you to."

"Why not?"

"I don't like killing things. Spiders, bugs, ants, anything. I can't help it."

"You're afraid."

"No I'm not."

"Yes you are."

"No I'm not."

"You are."

"What if I am?"

"You don't want to become a fairy. Girls don't kiss fairies. Fairies kiss other fairies."

I closed the window, turned out the bathroom light, then Gookus and I collapsed, me onto my own bed and Gookus onto the sleeping bag stretched out on the floor. We had trouble falling asleep; through the open air vent we heard raspy breathing coming from my parents' bedroom directly above mine.

"Know what that is?" Gookus asked.

"What what is?"

"That sound."

"Sure."

"What is it?"

"My mother snoring."

Gookus made the sound of a buzzer on a game show indicating the wrong answer.

"Then what is it?"

"Your father doing your mother."

"My father doing what to my mother?" I inquired, mildly alarmed.

"It—screwing."

"No way."

"Yes way. You can tell 'cause you can hear the bed squeak."

For a minute or two we stayed extraordinarily quiet but couldn't hear the bed squeak.

"Still, that's what it is," Gookus said.

"I don't believe you."

"Wanna go watch? I'll prove it to you. Or are you too much of a fairy?"

In our pajamas, in the dark, we crept upstairs, took turns looking through the keyhole of my parents' bedroom, and by the night-light watched my mother sleeping on the other side of the bed from my father. She lay on her back with her arms folded across her chest and one foot sticking out of the covers, heaving her entire body with every breath.

"They must have heard us coming and broke it off," Gookus said as he crawled back into the sleeping bag. "Wanna go back and check again? I swear I heard 'em doing it."

"You go if you want."

Gookus, disgusted, gave up and collapsed against the pillow. I remember what exquisite torture it was to know that this dangerous territory Gookus already seemed to have thoroughly staked out was, so far as I was concerned, not yet even on the horizon.

"Well, if they weren't doing it," Gookus wanted to know, "why was she breathing like that?"

"She has cancer."

"Get outta here."

"She's had it for years."

"Get outta here."

Gookus had sex, but I had death; I'd capped him.

"She'll probably have it a while longer," I said.

"And then?"

"She'll either get better or she won't."

"Jesus, Walt. I'm sorry. Really I am. I didn't know."

"Yeah."

"Nice face, though. She's got a really nice face."

The

War

on

Poverty

i

My mother gathered our family together in the living room to introduce our first and only maid to the rest of us, and while the hired help was changing into her uniform in the bathroom, my mother whispered, "Treat her with respect now. She's had a hard life. She lives in Watts. Be nice to her."

The Watts riots—or "rebellion," the term my mother preferred—had occurred that summer, and my parents now served on the board of virtually every civil rights organization: Youth Opportunity Board, Neighborhood Youth Corps, Operation Head Start, Work Experience Program. My mother was press director for a task force seeking to remove from office William Parker, chief of the LAPD, who, in the wake of the festivities, had been quoted as saying, "One person threw a rock. Then, like monkeys in a zoo, others started throwing rocks."

Virginia, the maid, walked out of the hallway bathroom, wearing a starched uniform. My mother turned around, squeezed Virginia's shoulder, and pushed her into the living room. The dog, a black-and-white mutt, barked.

"Virginia, this is my husband: Mr. Jaffe. You can call him Leonard."

"Hello."

"You can call him Leonard, Virginia."

"Yes, Mrs. Jaffe."

"Oh, I wish you wouldn't call me that. I asked you to call me Sylvia."

"I'd just as soon not."

"I guess we'll just have to give our friendship time to develop."

"Yes."

"Virginia, these are my children: Walt and Ellen."

Ellen didn't move from the broken chair she was sitting on, only nodded, politely smiled, but I stood up, and when I said hello, I felt pink palms, white fingernails, big black hands.

I could hear my mother show Virginia the cleaning closet in the back porch: "This is the vacuum cleaner. These are the attachments. This is the dustpan and broom. These are the rags. If you have any questions, any problems whatsoever, don't hesitate to ask me first thing."

Virginia lugged the vacuum cleaner past me and down the hallway to my parents' bedroom. My mother carried various plastic attachments in her arms—a round suction cup with bristles for hard-to-reach spots, a long flat piece for doing couches, and an extension cord—and said, "Here, Virginia, in case you need any of these things."

Virginia threw the plastic pieces on the bed and, according to my mother, plugged in the vacuum cleaner while my mother motioned with her arms and tried to talk above the noise, wondering whether the walls and the pictures on the walls shouldn't be dusted before she began vacuuming, whether the carpet beneath the bed couldn't be cleaned more thoroughly if the bed were pushed against the far wall, whether back and forth or at least across might not be more efficient than haphazardly sending the vacuum cleaner every which way, but Virginia ignored all this and over the sound of the machine shouted at her to move out of the way so she could get that spot.

After she'd cleaned the whole house, she was invited by my mother to have coffee and cookies with the rest of the family, but Virginia said no. She wanted to be paid and driven to the bus stop; she didn't want to nibble cookies.

"Please, Virginia," my mother said, "please join us."

Virginia relented, so for half an hour we told her how clean all the rooms were—the bathroom sparkled, the den looked good as new—while she stared at her plate of cookies and cold cup of coffee.

My mother insisted on driving her not just to the bus stop but all the way home. Before they got to the heart of Watts—to what were renamed Charcoal Alley Number One and Charcoal Alley Number Two—my mother said Virginia said: "Stop. This is where I live. It's not a mansion but not a shack, either."

My mother pulled out a ten and a twenty and said, "Keep—"

"That'll be thirty-two dollars."

"What?"

"Thirty-two dollars is my going rate, Mrs. Jaffe."

"But, Virginia, you only worked four and a half hours."

"My time is valuable."

"But, Virginia, I thought we'd said—"

"Thirty-two dollars, Mrs. Jaffe."

My mother returned from a task-force meeting to bad news from Virginia: when she was dusting my mother's open jewelry box, she realized that one of my mother's diamond earrings was missing. My mother said not to worry; it would turn up somewhere. Virginia put down her vacuum cleaner and my mother put down her briefcase. The two of them emptied the jewelry box on the bedspread, examining the collection piece by piece three times, and, when Virginia finally found the earring trapped beneath some felt, she exhaled with a relief so extreme as to constitute a witty parody of devotion.

Bus service was undependable and my mother almost enjoyed short stints on the Harbor Freeway, so she and Virginia evolved a system whereby my mother picked her up in the morning and drove her home in the afternoon. One morning, my mother picked up Virginia standing proudly in front of her house, dropped her off on our back porch, opened the door, and told her to please feel free about eating whatever she found in the fridge while our family walked over to Griffith Park. My mother had packed lunch and she carried the picnic basket. My father brought his camera and a paperback copy of *Look Homeward, Angel*. Ellen and I hunted for misdirected tennis balls and golf balls, then went swimming and took turns dunking each other. Later, we caught up with our parents for lunch. My mother sliced the bread, meat, and cheese, and poured the juice. My father told me not to eat so many cookies. Then we all walked slowly back home, but we couldn't get in because my mother wasn't able to find her keys and my father hadn't brought his. I crawled through the basement window, calling out to Virginia that it was only me.

She didn't answer—I figured she must have finished and gone home; the house was immaculate—so I made my way blithely toward the front door. Virginia popped out of the utility closet and said, "Boo!"

I screamed and fell over backwards, hitting my head on the dog's basket in the corner.

"Oh my," Virginia said, "such a treat to get a real *re-sponse* out of you folks."

ii

When they couldn't have children of their own, my aunt and uncle adopted a baby boy from Trinidad. They lived in Washington, D.C., where my uncle was a Nader's Raider specializing in nuclear-industry safety violations and my aunt was extremely active in environmental issues, which for a while seemed to consist primarily of co-organizing an annual "Earth Day" celebration in the capital and going hiking in the Blue Ridge Mountains. My adoptive cousin became, first, a commercial airplane pilot, then a policeman, then a Tae Kwan Do instructor—anything requiring a uniform. This is a fairly frequent about-face: do-gooders' sons desiring a regimented virility so long denied them. Once, when I was nine or ten, I called my cousin "Cassius Clay" because he bore a distinct resemblance to the boxer. I meant it as flattery. My aunt said, "We'd appreciate it if you didn't call Richard 'Cassius Clay,' Walt, since Richard is dark-skinned but he's only one-quarter black and it would only confuse him."

iii

> Neither the State nor any subdivision or agency thereof shall deny, limit, or abridge, directly or indirectly, the right of any person, who is willing or desires to sell, lease or rent any part or all of his real property, to decline to sell, lease or rent such property to such person or persons as he, in his absolute discretion, chooses.

This was the fearful language of Proposition 14, sponsored by the California Real Estate Association a year after Watts. Although the "No on 14" campaign had much catchier slogans ("Would you want your daughter to marry a realtor?" "Don't legislate hate") than the opposition did ("Rent or sell to whom you choose"), Proposition 14 won by a margin of two to one. Both my mother and father were extremely active in the No on 14 campaign—planning events, arranging speakers, writing pamphlets, preparing ads for newspaper, television, and radio—and they were crushed when this racist proposition passed overwhelmingly. Both the California Supreme Court and the U.S. Supreme Court ultimately repealed the amendment, but at the time my parents' only consolation was this: Darryl, a young man from Watts who had canvassed his heart out on the campaign, needed a place to stay and agreed to move into our den.

He wore an old-fashioned suit for a little party at our house: when he answered the door, someone's kid gave Darryl his windbreaker; when he bumped into an elderly woman in the living room, she asked him, "Where are the drinks?" He lost the key to the house, walked four miles in the rain to borrow my key, and was threatened with arrest when the vice-principal saw him strolling across the courtyard. If he stood still in stores, customers would ask him if he worked here, where men's shirts were, whether the sale applied to all fabrics. He was arrested for driving twenty-seven miles an hour in a twenty-five-mile-an-hour zone. At dinner, a friend of the family asked him whether he played any sports at Los Angeles City College (he was quite tall but completely un-coordinated). My mother prepared dishes such as black-eyed peas, grits, and Southern fried steak, which she thought might appeal especially to him but which neither he nor anyone else was able to swallow. My father talked to him about W.E.B. Du Bois and he said, "Who?" My sister tu-tored him in mathematics and told him he was hopeless when he said that, where 4x equals twenty-eight, x equals twenty-four. It was all so embarrassing and trite I don't know how he stayed with us as long as he did.

In a history course at LACC, Darryl met a sloe-eyed siren who was so unintelligent that by comparison Darryl sounded like W.E.B. Du Bois. He dropped out of school, got engaged, and told my family that he'd be moved out by the end of the week. My mother said they could live together in the guest room for as long as they wanted or needed to. They made so much noise my mother told him maybe he should move out by the end of the week. They found a third-floor walk-up near a twenty-four-hour convenience store. Both Darryl and Lisa had second thoughts before the ceremony, and friends discouraged them from getting married: Darryl, because she was so slow; Lisa, because he was black. Darryl's parents couldn't afford to drive all the way from Memphis to attend the wedding, so my parents substituted. Lisa's parents, overcome with emotion, cried throughout the ceremony. The marriage was a spectacular success until the end of the first year, when he became so bored with her that he went back to school, and the baby was given up for adoption.

Darryl continued to have trouble with mathematics, but he did well in his other courses, especially history, and after graduating from LACC he applied to Cal State Los Angeles and was accepted. Days he went to school, nights he bussed dishes, and after three years he earned a bachelor's degree, with distinction, in Afro-American history. The chairman of the department asked him to pursue graduate studies there, but he had his pick of the best schools in the country and went to almost the best of the best. I, too, went to almost the best of the best. I was a freshman when he was finishing his dissertation on W.E.B. Du Bois. I looked up Darryl in the student directory and we went out and got plastered and tried very hard to be sentimental about the past, but that wasn't how either of us felt and we were both excruciatingly tongue-tied when it came time to start trading amusing anecdotes.

iv

My friends and I were walking home from junior high school when one of us was hit in the leg with a rock. He clutched the back of his leg and fell to the ground while the rest of us picked up stones from a front-yard landscape and hid behind trees. Black boys waiting for their bus home continued to throw rocks at the white boy writhing in the street until he was able to scramble over to us. All the white boys threw rocks at the black boys, while I alternately hid my head in my hands and asked the boy whose leg was bleeding through his pants if he was all right. The black boys came closer, calling the white boys honkies and pussies and throwing rocks fast enough to kill. The white boys kept their ground, calling them niggers and jungle bunnies and returning the rocks until I stood in the middle of the street, waving my hands over my head and asking both sides, please, to stop hurting each other. White boys and black boys suddenly had a common cause: a hail of ammo was coming my way, and I ran zigzag into the early evening.

The
Heroic
Mode

Although the Greek Tragedy professor said that reading the play carefully, once, would probably be sufficient preparation for the quiz, I couldn't stop reading *Prometheus Bound* and also, for some reason, critical commentary upon it. I was a freshman and I loved how scholars felt compelled to criticize the play for not obeying certain Aristotelian dicta but how they were nevertheless helplessly drawn to "the almost interstellar silence of this play's remote setting," as one of them put it. I wrote my sister that, although our father pretended to be Prometheus, he was really only Io. I blurted out quotes to my friend Nina, with whom I was secretly infatuated.

"Walter, why are you studying so much?" Nina asked. "You're running yourself ragged. You know he said we could take the quiz before or after spring break. There's no reason to punish yourself."

"You must not have read the play," I said and proceeded to quote my favorite line: " 'To me, nothing that hurts shall come with a new face.' The admirable thing about Prometheus is that he accepts his fate without ever even hoping for another outcome."

"Yeah, maybe so, but at the end of the play he's still chained to a rock."

"There's a certain purity in basing your entire identity upon a single idea, don't you think? Nothing else matters except how completely I comprehend a drama written twenty-four hundred years ago. If I don't fully grasp each question, after a week of studying, I'll probably jump off the Caucasus," I said, referring to the mountains of the play and grabbing her arm. "I can sense some excitement."

"Shhh," she said, putting her finger over her lipsticked lips. "People are studying."

"You're as bad as the chorus of Oceanos's daughters, always telling Prometheus to stop pouting."

Nina thought I was kidding and laughed, shaking her head. I told myself I was kidding and tried to believe it. I felt as if I were a court jester parading around, to everyone's astonishment, in chinos and a turtleneck. I studied until five in the morning the day of the quiz. I fell asleep in my room and barely awoke in time for class, stumbling into the lecture hall. I filled two blue books in twenty minutes. My pen didn't leave paper. Whole speeches stormed from my mind. I wrote in immense handwriting, child's handwriting, out of control. I misidentified virtually every passage in the play but explicated them with such fevered devotion that the sympathetic teaching assistant gave me an A – .

. . .

I took a train from Providence to Washington, D.C., then a cab out into the suburbs, and when I appeared on her front porch in Bethesda, my aunt asked how long I'd been ill. "I groan for the present sorrow, I groan for the sorrow to come," I thought, "I groan questioning whether there shall come a time when He shall ordain a limit to my sufferings." I went into the bathroom to look at myself in the mirror and saw black circles around my eyes. I listened to my aunt tell my father over the phone how wonderfully I'd matured.

I secluded myself for most of the Easter vacation in my uncle's study. My uncle, the Nader's Raiders engineer, was away on a trip through the Northeast, checking out some new nuclear power plants. Nearly all the books in his study were technical, indecipherable, and of little interest to me— a big Aeschylus fan. Rummaging through desk drawers, I came across elaborate lists of domestic and secretarial errands for my aunt to perform and a few recent issues of *Penthouse,* which at the time I found extremely erotic because of its emphasis upon Amazonian women.

My uncle's office had a small record player and a stack of classical music. He had numerous different performances of Beethoven's Symphony Number 3, the so-called Heroic Symphony, and I found myself immersed, first, in all the liner notes. "Like Beethoven, Napoleon was a small man with a powerful personality," and Beethoven admired him, so when the French ambassador to Vienna suggested to Beethoven that he write a symphony about Bonaparte, Beethoven agreed. He was just about to send the finished score to Paris for Napoleon's official approval when he heard that Napoleon had proclaimed himself Emperor. Beethoven tore off the title page, which had only the word "Bonaparte" on it, and changed the dedication to "Heroic Symphony—composed to celebrate the memory of a great man." Beethoven is then supposed to have said, "Is he too no more than a mere mortal?" Beethoven was disappointed, in other words, to discover that Napoleon was human.

Why was a funeral march in the middle of the symphony? Why was the finale borrowed from the ballet *The Creatures of Prometheus?* Because—one commentator surmised—Beethoven "planned his symphony as a diptych, after the manner of his favorite book, *Plutarch's Lives,* in which every modern biography is paired with an antique one like it; thus the first two movements of the *Eroica* are about Napoleon and the second two about Prometheus." Oh, Prometheus. I knew, as I listened over and over again to the symphony, I'd felt elated and suicidal in exactly the same way before.

And the musicologists talking about Beethoven and Napoleon sounded eerily like the classicists discussing Prometheus or like me discussing the classicists discussing Prometheus: "What Beethoven valued in Bonaparte at the time of writing the *Eroica* was the attempt to wrest fate from the hands of the gods—the striving that, however hopeless, ennobles the man in the act," etc. I couldn't sleep at night because I couldn't get out of my head either the two abrupt gunshots in E-flat major which began the symphony or the trip-hammer orgasm of the coda, so I outlined an essay on the parallel and contrasting uses of water imagery in Aeschylus' *Oresteia* and O'Neill's *Mourning Becomes Electra.* Nina had suggested I adopt a "mythopoeic" approach to the paper. Instead, I circled every water image in both trilogies.

A friend of mine from high school was a freshman at Georgetown, so I called her up; I'd always wanted to get to know her better. I let the phone ring twice and hung up. I called again the next day, and the line was busy. The third time I called, she answered on the first ring, clearly expecting someone else. Her voice was newly inflected to underscore her International Relations major.

My aunt made breakfast for me every morning. We talked a lot. She asked me to define existentialism. She watched television and washed the dishes. I started agreeing with her.

This was all quite a while ago: the documentary film *Hearts and Minds* had recently been released. I drove into Georgetown to see it, and when I returned I sat in my aunt's kitchen, excoriating the racist underpinnings of all military aggression, but I was really thinking about only one scene: the moment when two U.S. soldiers, fondling their Vietnamese prostitutes, surveyed the centerfolds taped to the mirrored walls and, for the benefit of the camera, tried to imitate heroic masculinity.

The Gun in the Grass at Your Feet

Imagine, then, this situation.

What situation?

Answer honestly.

I will, Father.

Imagine three men standing together in a glade in the High Sierras.

Who are these people?

One of them is you, and the other two men are Pierce, the potential murderer, and Henkel, the potential victim.

Why is Pierce any more the potential murderer than Henkel is?

He holds a gun in his hand.

Ah.

Pierce—

What kind of gun?

What difference does it make?

I don't know, I just—

A pistol. A fast-loading little Army handgun.

Okay.

Pierce, standing to one side of you, points the gun directly at Henkel, who is standing on your other side. You're a few feet back from the line of fire.

The gun is loaded?

Yes, of course. Pierce does not know Henkel. This particular afternoon in the mountains is the first time he has ever seen him. No one knows why Pierce has chosen Henkel, of all people. Henkel is innocent. He has never done anything to harm Pierce. Nor does anyone know why Pierce is ready to commit murder.

I see.

Henkel strips to the waist, unbuckles his belt, and stands erect, with his eyes staring straight ahead at the thin barrel of the pistol.

Why doesn't he run away?

Pierce would kill him.

He might miss, though. Maybe he has poor aim.

He wouldn't miss. It would be impossible. They're standing five feet away from each other. And Pierce is a sharpshooter. From such close range he simply could not miss.

Do you still have a good eye?

What does that have to do with the situation?

You're right. I'm sorry.

Of course I still do.

Henkel simply stands there?

Right. You must accept as given the two facts of the situation: Henkel cannot flee and Pierce cannot miss. That's just the way it is.

Okay.

Say that with some enthusiasm.

Okay. Fine.

While Pierce aims the gun at Henkel's head and prepares to squeeze the trigger, Henkel, standing completely still, looks at you.

At me? Why is that?

Pierce has thrown the gun into the grass at your feet. Then he speaks.

What does he say?

Pick up the gun, Pierce says to you. Either pick up the gun or don't pick up the gun. Pick up the gun and shoot me or don't pick up the gun and watch me shoot Henkel.

Pierce will let me shoot him?

Yes.

What if I miss?

Impossible. You can't miss. He's standing five feet away from you. You couldn't miss if you tried.

But I need to know who these people are. What are they doing there?

Pierce has brought the three of you to the High Sierras for the express purpose of killing Henkel. Pierce is a dentist; Henkel, a grocer.

There must be some reason he chose Henkel.

None whatsoever. The only reason he chose Henkel was that he had absolutely no reason to choose him. It's a murder without motive or justification.

I'm afraid Pierce will kill me after he kills Henkel.

I assure you that won't happen. You have the chance to save a man who has done nothing wrong in his entire life, who distributes fresh fruit and vegetables at reasonable prices, and who, above all, is innocent. You have the chance to punish a man who has conceived a murder for his own amusement and who drills pain into children's teeth.

Don't turn Henkel into a martyr. He's a fool. He should never have gone out there with Pierce in the first place.

You're telling me that Pierce will bend down and pick up the gun in the grass at your feet and you'll just stand there. Pierce will squeeze the trigger, Henkel will breathe his last, and Pierce and you will walk away together out of the glade and into the sunlight.

I can't kill. I can't squeeze the trigger. I don't know how and I don't want to learn.

It makes no difference to you that Pierce is guilty and Henkel is innocent?

It does, but I can't be the one who decides who lives and who dies.

What are you talking about? You killed Henkel.

No I didn't. Pierce killed him.

Coward! Murderer!

Father, please.

Henkel lies there on the cold grass while Pierce and you go scot-free.

Please.

Murderer! Murderer!

A Brief Survey of Ideal Desire

Fathers and teachers,
I ponder "What is hell?"
I maintain that it is
the suffering of being
unable to love.

DOSTOEVSKY

Galleons laden with jewelry and threatened by pirates sailed through treacherous seas in the gold-on-blue design of Walt's rabbit-feet pajamas. He would hold the strap attached to his rocking horse's ears and mouth, lifting himself onto the little leather saddle. One cracked green glass eye shone out of the right side of Silver's head. His mouth, once bright red and smiling, had chipped away to a tight-lipped, unpainted pout. His nose, too, was bruised, with gashes for nostrils. Silver had a brown mane, which, extending from the crown of his head nearly to his waist, was made up of Walt's grandmother's discarded wigs glued to the wood. Wrapping the reins around his fist, Walt would slip his feet into the square stirrups that hung from the horse's waist. Walt would bounce up and down to set Silver in motion, lean forward, press his lips to the back of his horse's rough neck, and exhort him to charge. When Silver pitched forward, Walt would scoot up toward the base of the horse's spine, and when Silver swung back, Walt would let go of the leather strap and lean back as far as he could. Walt would make the rocking horse lurch crazily toward the far wall by squeezing his knees into wood and jerking his legs forward. Then he'd twist his hips and bounce until it felt warm under him, bump up against the smooth surface of the seat until his whole body tingled. He'd buck back and forth so it hurt, in a way, and he wouldn't know what to do with this ache.

From age eleven until age fifteen Walt did little else but play basketball all afternoon and evening, and when it grew too dark to see the rim, he played by the light of the street lamp. He played on school teams, on temple teams, in pickup games, for hours alone, with friends, against friends, with people he'd never seen before and never saw again, with middle-aged men wearing college sweatshirts who liked to keep their hands on his ass as they guarded him, with friends' younger brothers who couldn't believe how good he was, with UCLA Bruins keeping in shape during the summer who told him he might make it, with coaches who told him the future of their jobs rested on his performance, with the owners of a pornographic bookstore who asked him if he wanted to appear in an art film, with his father, who asked him whatever happened to the concept of teamwork. He wore leather weights around his ankles, taking them off only in bed, so his legs would be strong and he would be able to jump as high as his black teammates could. He read every available book on technique, every biography of the stars. He jumped rope: inside, around the block, up stairs, walking the dog. He played on asphalt, in playgrounds, in gyms, in the street, in the backyard, in his mind, in rain, in winds that ruled the ball, beneath the dead dry heat of burning sun.

Walt ascended two flights of cement stairs, then knocked on the door, which had an engraving of Venus straddling an aqueduct. A large blonde lady, wearing high heels made of glass, opened the door. "Hello," she said, aspirating heavily, "and welcome to A Touch of Venus." She handed him a glass of white wine and a poorly typed page, which was encased in plastic and which said:

A Touch of Venus—The Most in Massage

1. The Basic. Masseuse fully clothed. No oils, no scents. 1 drink. Access to billiard table. Very relaxing. Fifteen minutes. $20.

2. The Rubdown. Masseuse clothed in underwear. Oils, no scents. 2 drinks. Access to billiard table, whirlpool, shower massage. Highly sensitizing. Twenty minutes. $30.

3. The Total Massage. Masseuse clothed in black underwear. Oils, scents. 3 drinks. Access to billiard table, whirlpool, shower massage, screening room, Jacuzzi. Extremely refreshing. Thirty minutes. $50.

4. A Little Bit of Heaven. Masseuse topless. Asian oils, Parisian scents. Unlimited drinks. Access to billiard table, whirlpool, shower massage, screening room, Jacuzzi, lemon creme facial. Quite exciting. Forty-five minutes. $75.

5. Ecstasy. Masseuse topless and bottomless. Asian oils, Parisian scents. Unlimited drinks. Access to billiard ta-

ble, whirlpool, shower massage, screening room, Jacuzzi, sauna, lemon creme facial. Hot towel wrap. Champagne bubble bath. Discount card for return visits. Fulfilling. One hour. $100.

Walt was astonished that so many of the details with which he had conjured up this scenario proved to be accurate: black leather couches, thick red carpet, low lighting, disco music, shiny wood paneling, coffee tables on which were spread recent copies of *Penthouse.* "So," his hostess said, "what'll it be—Ecstasy, A Little Bit of Heaven, Total Massage . . ." Her voice trailed off. It seemed clear that anything short of ecstasy was mere flirtation. "Ecstasy," Walt said. He paid her with money he'd saved from his job as a stock boy at a clothing store, and she took him on a tour of the building, which used to be the fire department, she said, before it was converted. Walt thought back to a time when big, happy men were polishing trucks and waiting around to be heroes. She held him by the arm and told him to relax as they walked through the lounge, in which the other masseuses were watching a faded color film of four people fucking, then gave him a white bathrobe and a key to a locker and told him to change into—the phrase was meant to be excruciatingly erotic, and it was—"something more comfortable." The sauna, the whirlpool, the shower massage (whatever that was), the Jacuzzi, the champagne bubble bath, all this stuff was in the basement of the ex-firehouse; Walt was instructed to slide down the golden pole and amuse himself for a while and come upstairs when he was ready. He was ready right then, of course; he hadn't paid a hundred dollars to take a bath by himself, and as he climbed into the sauna and sat on the wooden bench, he tried and failed to imagine anything worse than being in the basement of a converted fire station on Sunday morning. He consoled himself with the thought that, before he left, at least he would have sinned. When he went upstairs, he sat in a director's chair, watching the movie and thumbing through magazines, and one by one the employees offered themselves to him. His hostess asked him to play pool with her, a short redhead sat next to him and watched the movie for a couple of minutes, and a skinny woman with black hair wrapped high around her head like tangled snakes brought him a drink. He was supposed to give a little ticket that he held in his hand to the woman of his dreams, but instead he got up and gave the ticket to the only masseuse who was not in any way appealing or exciting or terrifying. She was shy and Walt had to force the ticket into her hand to get her to look up. She led him into a room and told him to take off his bathrobe. He lay face down on a table in the middle of the room and she rubbed him from head to toe. He stared at a large square mirror positioned on the floor in such a way that he could see her. Most of what she did tickled, so he thought about other things to keep from laughing. It wasn't arousing, and after a while he flipped over on his back, sat up, and complained. She said this was a legitimate massage parlor and they didn't do that kind of thing here. "We'll be quiet," he assured her and offered her a fifty-dollar tip, but she said she wasn't for sale. He lunged toward her; she stepped back and hurried out the door before he could stop her. He ran out of the room and down the stairs to the locker room, changed into his clothes, then left by the back exit. The rest of the money in his wallet was gone. When he got outside and into the sunlight, Walt felt the way he had felt the year before upon leaving the theater after seeing a pornographic movie for the first time: sentimental, thrilled by the mundanity of cracks in the sidewalk and flowers, and repelled by the prospect of physical love.

. . .

Walter and Nina had remained in bed until three o'clock in the afternoon, which was twenty minutes after he was supposed to have boarded a Bonanza bus to Logan Airport, because Nina, wearing only a pair of warm socks and very warm mittens, wanted to squeeze the fat in his back with her wool hands and dig into his legs with her warm wool feet so that he would feel like he was being devoured by a ferocious little lion and return as quickly as possible and think of no one and nothing else while he was away. Every time Nina got even near him, he started sneezing, and he was one of those people who, rather than make a quick little ka-choo into a handkerchief, not only neglect to carry a handkerchief but feel compelled to blow coagulations of snot into the atmosphere, into their hands, drippy and yellow, onto whatever is around them at the moment. What was around Walter at the moment was Nina's bed sheet, which she had just washed and dried so that she and Walter would have a clean, white surface to slide around on their last night together. She was so disgusted by the way he shook the snot off his hands into the wastebasket and blew his nose with the cord to his bathrobe that she got out of bed, standing with her mittens on her hips and her socked feet on the floor next to the electric heater, and quoted back to him the analogy he always liked to make between the itch in the nose and desire, between phlegm on the floor and fulfillment. "It really empties you out, right?" she said. "Tell me, sweetheart, does it also make you feel sad?" Walter thought he was sneezing because he'd finally developed an allergy to Nina, whereas Nina, who had learned all about psychosomatic disorders when she was in analysis, assumed he was sneezing because he'd developed an allergy to his family, whereas the truth was that he had developed an allergy to the dust he'd encountered the night before, searching for his suitcase in the basement. While he stuffed the suitcase with what few articles of light clothing he still owned, she started the car, an old Peugeot the color of pool water, which her father had given her after the mechanic said he'd never be able to stop the ping in the motor; she drove ten miles faster than anyone else on cleared and sanded 95 North all the way to the airport. They made it in plenty of time. "I'll miss you. I love you," he said to reassure Nina, who had started glowering when he glanced at the cover of *Club International* magazine in the gift shop before doing whatever was the opposite of deplaning. "You love your free detachable calendar of Miss Cunt of the Month," she said and kissed him good-bye until he started sneezing again.

"I can see why you're a Miss Nude USA regional finalist," Walter imagined writing the woman whose ad was placed in the back of *Club*. "You have beautiful long silky blue-black hair, a perfect pout, and a gorgeous body. Please send me the color photos you mentioned of yourself in fur, leather, lingerie, garter belt, and heels. Thank you. Payment enclosed."

The ending of James Joyce's story "The Dead" was usually interpreted as Gabriel Conroy's unambiguous, transcendental identification with universal love and human mortality, but to Walter it seemed more plausible to read the last page or so as an overwritten passage that conveyed emotional deadness taking refuge in sentimentality. "Generous tears filled Gabriel's eyes. He had never felt like that himself towards any woman, but he knew that such a feeling must be love." Gabriel was thinking about the passion of his wife's ex-suitor, but the word "generous" appeared—to Walter, at least—to suggest Gabriel's confusion of self-pity with selfless love. Walter figured that, if Joyce had meant the last sentence of the story to be truly beautiful, he certainly wouldn't have used "falling faintly" and "faintly falling" within four words of each other. This repetition created discord at the very climax of the rising hymn so that, even as Gabriel believed he was liberating himself from egotism, his language for compassion was self-conscious and solipsistic. Neither in memory nor fantasy was he capable of imagining union, completion, or even shared intimacy. That was Walter's interpretation.

Sudden

Affection

The last two weeks of every summer they rented a cabin until one year at high tide, during a storm in the middle of winter, waves crashing beyond the backshore loosened the shabby foundation of the house, and their castle on the water collapsed, drifting off to sea in splinters. This wasn't the year of the storm, high winter waves, the splintered sea: this was before the bad weather.

Every summer they came to this final fort at the edge of the Pacific, hoping to find a cove cut into the crags where they could stretch out, close their eyes, and let the sun peel away their aches and pains. And yet every summer they were unhappy. They argued with themselves, with each other, with their children. Out of such conflicts, sand castles were crushed and summer romances were ruined. This summer

would be different. This summer they wouldn't listen to—
they wouldn't even hear—anything other than the soft flush
of the sea.

They came, this family of four, happily carrying bundles
of clothes and towels from their overheated car to their run-
down shack. Driving from the center of the city to the coast,
they had battled the traffic and one another all morning.
Now they were here. They were tired of the smog. They
wanted to breathe pure ocean air. Mrs. Jaffe was skinny and
weak. She carried nothing and told her husband and children what to do. They followed her and said, "What next?"

"This basket," she said, "that suitcase, this box. Hold it
from the bottom. With two hands."

She coughed and smoked (to her family's amazement and
chagrin) and coughed, and they carried. Up and back they
marched from the car to the house under her direction,
walking slowly to the doorstep as they balanced things and
trudged their way through the sand, then ran back to the
car to get more swim gear, more blankets, more food.

It wasn't their house. It didn't belong to them. It belonged to a man whom Mr. Jaffe owed many favors but who
was willing to let Mr. Jaffe pile up more debts. Mr. Jaffe
hadn't paid last summer's rent and had no way to pay this
summer's. Theirs was the last one in a long line of squat
white houses that faced the beach and sat above the rocks.
The paint was flaking; the windows were broken and boarded
up. The front porch was gutted. Wild grass grew high as the
head all the way around the house. It was a miserable place,
and inside was worse.

They left everything in a heap in the hallway. In a tiny
bedroom that had plastic swordfish tacked to the walls, Mr.
Jaffe changed into his swimsuit, which was red like coral.
Since the surgery, Mrs. Jaffe was shy about being seen naked, especially by her husband, so she undressed in the bath-

room, where she stood on warped wooden slats that were supposed to serve as the shower floor. Her splotched skin was sensitive to sun. She wore a white hat that curved down in front and up in back and had pink polka dots scattered like a disease over the brim. She also wore dark green sunglasses and a long-sleeve turtleneck. Underneath she wore an ugly old swimsuit. Mr. Jaffe did jumping jacks in front of the mirror in the bedroom. Even she admired his body. He awoke at six every morning and ran through the city streets. He was in excellent shape. But he wasn't a strong man in any way that mattered to her. He was weak.

She loved her children. She lavished extravagant attention upon both of them. She brushed Ellen's hair and tied her swimming suit and scratched her back, laced and knotted the drawstring to Walt's trunks and played catch with him. It was a beach ball and very light, but she threw underhand.

"Throw it harder," Walt said.

"I'm trying," she said.

"Throw it harder."

"That's enough, Walt."

"Higher."

"Shut your mouth."

"So here we are," Mrs. Jaffe said to no one in particular and no one in particular responded. She reiterated her happiness, her anticipation of family fun. The children nodded and Mr. Jaffe pecked her on the cheek. That wasn't what she wanted. She wanted sudden affection, a tear in the eye, a sob cut short in the throat. She pulled them close to her and hugged them, blowing smoke in their faces. Ellen didn't like smoke and coughed. Mr. Jaffe carried towels and blankets in one hand and an umbrella in the other. Walt carried an inner tube and the beach ball. Ellen swung the picnic basket. Mrs. Jaffe held matches and her pack of cigarettes.

They walked through the wild grass and on rough, round rocks. Only Mrs. Jaffe had remembered to wear shoes. She wore white tennis shoes with pretty laces; the others bounded quickly across the rocks. She no longer had any endurance, and the slightest movement, the most polite gesture at exercise, caused her to wheeze and go blue in the face. Even this little stroll made her heart race and she stopped to catch her breath.

"Slow down," she said. She needed a child's hot hand to hold, but they had all run ahead of her and were making their way, in single file and with steady steps, down the cliff that rose up out of the backshore.

"Come back here," she said.

They threw everything onto the sand and jumped the last few feet to the beach. She stood at the edge of the cliff and nearly lost her balance. She looked down and could see no footholds cut into the rock. It looked so far, so steep. She shook her head and started to walk back to the beach house, but Mr. Jaffe held out his arms and said, "Slide down, dear: I'll catch you."

Mr. Jaffe was strong, and although she knew he would catch her, she was still afraid. She didn't look forward to the bumpy ride down the mountain or the tingle she would feel in the balls of her feet when she hit bottom. A sandy path wound through the cliff, and her husband insisted she slide down it.

"I'll go back to the house and rest," she said.

"Slide down, honey," he said.

She sat in the sand at the edge of the path, then pushed off. Down she went. She knew she looked ridiculous— bouncing toward the beach, kicking her feet, waving her hands, screeching. When she got to the bottom, Mr. Jaffe's feet were planted in the sand and his arms were stretched out to catch her. She was very light; he caught her easily.

She collapsed in his arms. He held her tight until she stopped shaking and sweating, then stood her on her feet. They walked on in search of a cove that would protect them from the wind.

Walt and Ellen ran ahead while Mr. and Mrs. Jaffe walked arm in arm and talked about the glare of the full sun sitting on the water, the cawing sound the sea gulls made. She didn't like to see girls in bikinis kissing inebriated boys. She thought Ellen might get the wrong idea. She hated the families that brought loud radios and babies in cribs to the beach, the funny little men selling soft drinks who walked up right next to you. She liked the idea of the beach and talked and dreamed about it every year, but she never actually liked the beach itself. It was always too crowded.

The children found a cove cut deep into the cliff, which would protect her from the wind and other people and the water. She was out of breath by the time she got there. She collapsed on a towel and wrapped a blanket around herself. Mr. Jaffe told her to close her eyes and sleep; he and the children were going swimming and would be back in a while, but she didn't want to be left alone, so she took off her turtleneck sweater and long pants. She stood, shivering, in her navy blue bathing suit.

Walt rolled the inner tube and kept tapping it until it got out of his control and bounded down to the waterline, where it spun to a muddy stop. Mr. Jaffe chased after him. Mrs. Jaffe told Mr. Jaffe to warn Walt about the undertow, although she had little sense really what the undertow was or what it looked like or when and where it existed.

Mr. Jaffe let go of her hand. He crawled around in the water and stepped on rocks until he had dog-paddled far enough out so that he could swim. He swam around awhile, then pulled her into shallow water. She felt like she'd forgotten how to swim and started to sink. She flapped her arms and called for help, but Mr. Jaffe was swimming underwater toward the dock and the children were sailing out toward sea on the inner tube. Straight down she went and saw nothing but dark green. Salt water stung her eyes, filled her lungs. As she fell deeper toward the ocean floor, she thought no one would save her; they'd bring her up in a burlap bag; at least it would be cleaner and faster this way. But one of the vendors swam out to get her, and after a brief struggle was able to tow her back to shore, pulling her out of the ocean onto the beach. He lay down on top of her and breathed into her blue mouth. She exhaled salt water, cigarette tar, and portions of breakfast and lunch. She squirmed in the sand. Mr. Jaffe came out of the water and asked if she was all right. The vendor asked if she'd like a soft drink. "No charge," he said.

Northern

Light

Hail falls Tuesday afternoon while Nina and I walk through the Live Free or Die art gallery in Portsmouth, looking for work that "pushes beyond boundaries" into . . . into what? Into "a personal, experimental phase." Is all interesting painting just a formal experiment that succeeds? One of us thinks so; the other mumbles maybe not. Some colors aren't too terribly vivid. We're for "a little strong, intense maturity." But "intensity of color," *plus* composition. Some things look trapped in genre, decoration, like exercises, almost as if they've been done for class. Go past facade to personality. Do not collect . . . art? Art is the "axe that breaks the frozen sea within us." We've heard that a thousand times. Up here, though, even the opposite of the pathetic fallacy turns into just another weather report.

Lies

Before my family went out to dinner, my father asked me, "Why aren't you wearing your good sweater?"

"It doesn't match what I'm wearing."

I was wearing a black sock, a dark blue sock with a hole in the big toe, good black shoes, checked blue pants, a striped green shirt, a dinner jacket, and an unknotted tie.

"You look a mess," he said. My mother and sister giggled compassionately.

"Sorry."

"Go downstairs and find a pair of socks that match, black pants, a white shirt. And fix your tie."

I put on a new pair of thick black socks, black pants, and a clean white shirt, combed my hair, knotted my tie, ran back upstairs, and when I returned, he said, "Where is it?"

"Where is what?"

"Your good sweater."

"Downstairs," I said.

"Bring it up."

I went back to my room, pulled out all my dresser drawers and coat hangers, even looked under the bed, but all I could find was my second-best sweater—a frayed brown turtleneck, which I brought up when he called down to me that he didn't wish to be late on my account.

I said, "Here: here it is."

"That's not your good sweater."

"Let's go. We'll be late. This is good enough."

"Where's your good sweater, the gold one with the brass buttons?"

"I don't know."

"You don't know?"

"I'm sure it's around. Let's go. I'll find it when we get back."

"We'll find it right now."

My sister sat down on a couch in the living room and read magazines, my mother went into the kitchen to eat fruit, and my father stormed downstairs, cursing me. I trailed after him and assured him the sweater would turn up. He, too, went through all my drawers, all my hangers, and when he didn't find the sweater, the good gold one with brass buttons, he sat me down on the bed and said, "You lost that sweater. Your grandfather worked hard to give you that sweater. You lost it, didn't you?"

"Yes, I did. I'm sorry."

"Where did you lose it?"

"I don't know. Somewhere. I have no idea."

He smacked me across the face and then said, "You'll never lie to me again."

"I won't," I said.
"Never again."
"I won't."

As I was getting ready to leave for school, packing my lunch, collecting my books, putting on my sweater, my father asked me if, after breakfast, I'd brushed my teeth.

I nodded, smiled, and blew cool, fresh breath up toward the ceiling.

"Good," he said, "but don't leave yet." He quickly left the kitchen and bounded down the stairs to my bathroom.

"I'll be late. I have to go."

He emerged at the head of the stairs, triumphantly holding my toothbrush in his hand.

"Your toothbrush is dry."

"So?"

"You didn't brush."

"I dried it with a towel."

He looked at me until I admitted I hadn't brushed my teeth.

For six months I brushed my teeth three times a day, used dental floss at night, ate barrels of apples, no candy, drank gallons of milk, then saw a dentist who told me he'd never seen so much plaque in his life; I had three cavities and would have false teeth by the time I was thirty if I kept up like this. I pushed the polishing brush out of my mouth and threw a tantrum until my father came over during his lunch break to take me home and show me how to brush up and down rather than across.

Gookus talked to the clerk, asking him questions about his job—the hours, the pay, whether he liked working in a toy store—while I stuffed plastic-wrapped packs of National League baseball cards into my jacket and coat pockets. The clerk worked Saturday, all day, and weekday nights from six to closing at ten; he wasn't at liberty to say how much he was paid other than it was a fair wage for the work he did; and, yes, he very much enjoyed selling plastic dolls and stuffed turtles to little children. Gookus nodded and waved, and he and I walked quickly out of the store when the clerk turned around to get a stalled electric racing car back on track. That night I stayed awake until everyone else in my house was asleep, then ran out to the backyard, where I shredded the stolen cards into garbage barrels. After saving up money for months from my allowance and small jobs, I placed twenty dollars in an envelope, rode my bicycle downtown, and slipped the envelope, with "Consider this a gift" scrawled on the front, under the glass at Tabler's Toyland.

I played handball with a graceful fourth-grader named Carol Cummings, and when the big red rubber ball bounced off the cement wall and flew between us, I let it go over my head, held her by the shoulders, and kissed her on the mouth. She neither liked it nor disliked it, but instead chased down the bouncing ball, washed out her mouth in the water fountain, and told her friends. I bragged about the event to my father, who when he heard Carol's last name not only asked me what was the matter with Leanne Gurevitch but told me I shouldn't be playing with girls.

Seven years later he asked me what was the matter with Leanne Gurevitch and told me I should be spending more time with girls. Carol Cummings grew up to be a very sexy acidhead who drove her car to the edge of a cliff overlooking Laurel Canyon, and then, to stop the snake crawling around inside her mind, jumped. I was in bed with Leanne Gurevitch, and when she asked me what I was thinking about I said, "Nothing."

"Nothing?" she said. "You must have been thinking about something."

"No, nothing. Go back to sleep."

She said: "Any interpersonal relationship is frustrating for me unless both people are absolutely honest with each other and hide none of their vulnerability."

"Carol Cummings," I said, and Leanne cried, got off me, got up, got dressed, and left the room.

Concerning the owner of a used-bicycle store I said, "Maybe we can jew him down."

Doug said, "I never thought I'd hear you say that."

"You say it all the time."

"Yes," Bradley said, "but he's not—"

"It doesn't mean anything to me. I don't believe in it," I said. "It's only my parents who are Jewish."

For them, for Bradley and Doug I said it, but from me they didn't want to hear it.

"Then you are, too," Doug said.

"I'm not."

"You are what your parents are," Bradley said. "That's all there is to it."

At dinner that night I turned to my father and asked, "Will you promise you'll forgive me for what I've done?"

"What have you done?"

"You must promise first."

"No, you must tell me first."

My sister and mother stopped eating, put down their glasses and forks, and listened.

"Doug was going to buy a used bicycle and I said maybe we could jew the store owner down."

My sister gasped.

My father said, "*Acch,* some son," then asked me to leave the table.

I said I'd rather finish eating my dinner.

In my room I sulked until I heard my father's footsteps. I opened the Old Testament and began reading, but he told me to put it away and quit faking.

"You're not my son," he said.

"What do you mean?"

"I'm a Jew. You aren't."

"I am! I am!"

"You aren't. I can't tell you how ashamed you've made me."

"They're my friends. I want them to like me. I want to talk the way they do."

"They talk like that?"

"All the time."

"You're forbidden to visit with either of them again."

"But they're my friends."

"They're your enemies."

On a damp Sunday afternoon I watched various boy-friends of Gookus' older sister break all twenty-four windows of a classroom that faced the teachers' parking lot. One of them was so proud and naive he told Gookus' sister, and she was so scared and confused she placed an anonymous phone call to the principal, telling him not who broke the windows but who witnessed the crime. A corpulent man with a poor complexion, Mr. Hemley asked me into his office and then asked me how I, Chief of Traffic Patrol, could have neglected to tell him of the incident. I said I had no idea what he was talking about, and he asked me to think about it and come back tomorrow. I called up Gookus, who told me that his sister's ex-boyfriends threatened to hang him from the lemon tree outside his house if I supplied the principal with their names. I told Gookus not to worry. The next morning, during recess, I went into Mr. Hemley's office and told him I wasn't on the school grounds Sunday and had no idea who had broken the windows. He stood up and waddled over to where I was sitting. "Are you sure?" he asked.

"Yes," I said and nodded.

"You're sure you're not lying?"

"Yes."

"You know that lying is wrong?"

"Yes."

"That liars are punished?"

"Yes."

"Have your parents told you never to tell a lie?"

"Yes."

"Always to tell the truth?"

"Yes."

"And you're being honest with me?"

"Yes."

"Will you tell me who broke the windows?"

"No."

He breathed in to remove his belt.

The
Moon,
Falling

The moon burned and we hiked on, up hills, down hills, farther into the recesses of the mountain. The moon was brilliant. Luminous even. Nina said it was a full moon. I agreed. That we were lost. I agreed. I told her not to worry. She asked me, please, to stop patronizing her. Nina didn't like the idea of being lost. I, obviously, reveled in it.

She asked me to promise we would stop at the first clearing to which we came. I'm tired, she said, you have to respect that. I told her I did; I was tired, too; sleep was inevitable and natural, like the moon. I wanted to remove the moon, rebel against sleep. I wanted to hike until the moon faded, until the sun rose, until my backpack slipped off my shoulders.

Nina cluttered the sunroom, the kitchen, the bathroom, the bedroom with plants. She played music for the plants on a cheap stereo. Like a child she loved Mozart, Brahms. She talked to the plants. Nights, naked, she walked around the house, spilling water, reading liner notes. The plants begged for more water. Dry dirt caked. Dead leaves crumbled. I flooded the plants. Don't, she said. Hanging plants dripped water. Potted plants toppled over. Soil became mud. Roots stretched like legs. Leaves turned into huge hands. Hanging plants swayed. You'll ruin them, she said, leave them alone. I bought records like candy. Mahler. Nothing else, only Mahler. Only the symphonies. I turned up the volume all the way. The plants sprouted up like arms, brought the ceiling down a foot or two. The plants took over the house, dominated rooms. The sunroom was transformed into a greenhouse. Nina said she felt suffocated by the plants, that they were out of control. She threw all of them out, then played Mozart, early Mozart, very quietly.

A clearing, Nina said. I agreed, although I was clearly disappointed. A place to sleep, she said. Yes, I said. We ran downhill like goats. She tripped, tasted dirt. I licked topsoil off her mouth. I swallowed earth. I spat out pebbles and dry terrain.

At the bottom of the hill we caught our breaths, absorbed the soft summer night, listened to water lapping. The river was wider and deeper than I thought it would be. Many things turn out that way. Nina, for instance. She said the water was filthy. Like a child I blew bubbles. I looked into the river, stared at murky water. Nina recounted the well-known Narcissus myth.

On another hike, in a secluded glade, surrounded by woods and the deep dark verdant shadows of cypress trees,

I played with the camera, adjusted the f-stop, twisted the black plastic strap. I undressed Nina in my mind. I thought about the softness of infinity, the violence of the close-up. I thought about undressing Nina. We don't have much sunlight left, I said. Shadows splashed across her face like paint. I read the light meter, tinkered with the f-stop. She made a pile of her clothes like laundry. She stood in the shade, folding her arms across her breasts. Put your arms down, I said. I feel naked, she said. You should, I said. I put the camera down, jumped out of my clothes. Better? I said. Yes, she said. I looked into the viewfinder: her arms were pinned to her bare legs like pickets. Sun angled through the trees, throwing my light reading off. Take off your glasses, I said, they refract light. No, she said, I can't see without them. There's glare, I said. I don't care, she said. The rhyme gave rise to laughter, to frolic, to my ripping her glasses off her face. I spoke of the poetry of blindness, the clarity of an oblique vision, our need for distortion. Give me back my glasses, she said. Shadows cut off the sun, stretched like ladders. Step out of the shadows, I said. Hands on bony hips, Nina walked out of the penumbra, sprawled out on the grass, chewed blades like a cow, spread her legs, rocked, fingered herself, arched her back like a cat. Better? she said. Yes, I said, hold it. I toyed with the range finder. Shadows sprayed her body like a water hose. I turned the f-stop to 2.8. I switched the shutter speed to $1/25$th of a second. It hurts, she said. I straddled her, crouched down, turned the camera vertically, focused. It hurts, she said. I spoke of the need, now and then, to suffer. I photographed through her body: I ducked between her legs and shot from her thighs to her face. Shadows fell like walls.

The river stretched itself out in front of us for years, wound its way through meadows, trees, bushes for as far as we could see in either direction. It presented itself to us like a broken arm, some nagging ugly contorted barrier. I threw our sleeping bags and backpacks, one at a time, onto the flat land of the empty dark field on the other side of the river. The backpacks clanked like prisoners. The sleeping bags flew like bullets. I ran to the foot of the hill behind me, stared up at triangular acres. The moon receded, climbed higher into the black sky, turned down its light, waited for the stars to dance. Don't go leaping over the river, Nina called, athletics repulse me.

In the pastels of early morning, on quiet empty black tar courts I served yellow tennis balls and she swung at air. I rushed the net, made chalk cough. I smashed cross-court shots at wicked, improbable angles. I sliced drop shots that bounced back onto my side of the court. I arched lobs that tickled the sky, landing inches inside the back line. I served hard, like a cannon, deep, into corners. You serve too hard, Nina said. She held her tennis racquet like a guitar. She hit backhands with two hands, spun around, lost her balance. She played in a white tennis dress. Emily Dickinson was buried in a white casket. Every other game we exchanged sides, slurped orange juice, kissed, intertwined racquets like serpents' heads, like hands, tugged at shorts. Don't, she said, I'm trying to concentrate. She concentrated. Like an athletic genius she concentrated. We played hundreds of games. She rarely won a point. I aimed for the bottom of the net and she won a game. She danced around the court and flung her racquet into the trees. She kissed me until I could taste the salt of her sweat. She gripped me like the handle of her racquet. I let you win, I said. I won, she said. I let you. You didn't. I did. She asked if she could see my racquet for a second, took out her nail clippers, and started sawing diagonally.

Don't jump, she said. I wasn't committing suicide. I was jumping over a river—shallow stream of murky water. I crouched low, felt light, felt bounce and spring in my legs. I wanted to land on dry earth, open up my sleeping bag, connect zippers with Nina. The moon twisted around like a dangling yo-yo. I clenched my fists, tugged at dirt, ran hard. Nina waved her hands, shook me off. You'll kill yourself, she said. The river was as wide as two tables. I was willing to risk it. She looked away, hid her face from the moon. As I neared the river my feet chopped at the ground like piano keys. I bounced off the last clump of earth before the river and lifted.

Arms outstretched, hands clapping air, stomach tight as a fist, I lifted. As if I were gliding forward in a swing I kicked my legs out ahead of me. I savored altitude, flight, proximity to the moon. As if I were riding a bicycle I pedaled air. Air led to earth, below me was water. The gravitational pull of the moon brought me down. And yet I made it. My right foot landed on level ground; my left foot, on the steep bank. I lunged forward, lost my balance. As I slid down the hill, belly up, I clutched crazily after rocks, twigs, things to hold on to. I slipped into the scummy edge of the river. I rolled away from the water like a crocodile into mud. I scrambled up the hill onto flat land, took off my wet shoes and socks, my soaked pants. Otherwise I was bone-dry.

Nina laughed. It was the kind of event that entertained her. She thought I was clumsy. She thought I had no sense of myself in relation to things around me. The things around me at the moment were weeds, rocks, backpacks, sleeping bags, clumps of bushes. I felt in union with them. With all of them, with each of them. In touch.

I loped around the kitchen like a gazelle, making a lavish breakfast in honor of Nina's birthday. These are dessert forks, she said, thumbing the Sunday paper, twanging the fork like a Jew's harp. I ignored her. The distinction seemed spurious. A fork is a fork, I thought. You shovel food with it. I patted the omelets, threw cold sesame bagels into the oven. Like a magician I switched forks. Like a gourmet I made breakfast. I poured milk, stirred orange juice, boiled water. Coffee, I said. Tea, she said. I whipped out tea bags like condoms. She folded the paper around her like a dressing room, occasionally poked her head out over the headlines, lost herself in new places to travel, new marriages, new books. Like a waiter I served omelets, crisp bagels. Like a fountain I spilled orange juice, tea, coffee. I slapped butter on a plate. These forks are dirty, she said. Fuck the forks, I said, eat with your hands. I pushed omelets past my face, swallowed bagels like sugar doughnuts, drank coffee, orange juice, cold milk. You're a glutton, she said. A slob, she explained, crumpling her newspaper. I rubbed my finger in butter, smeared her lips, kissed her until I thought I smelled smoke. My God, Walter, Nina said. The oven's on.

The moon turned on its side, nosed its way into oblivion. The moon, alone, bored with its own waning light, surrounded itself with stars. I couldn't see Nina on the other side of the river. I clapped my hands, called to her. Nina, I said. Nina, Nina. She howled like a dog. I'm not a dog, she said, don't you dare clap your hands at me. I applauded. I whistled. Come on, I said, jump over the river. I clucked my tongue. I snapped my fingers. Across the river she yelled at me.

Nina fed her dog the morning mail. She threw a rubber ball at its nose. Now and then she walked the animal, wrapping the leash around her wrist like a bracelet. She rubbed its black nose in its own shit. The dog, in heat, chased a Great

Dane. On the front lawn, at night, beneath Nina's window, a Great Dane and Nina's dog copulated. The Great Dane pranced away like a pimp. A few seconds later, months before it could have puppies, Nina's dog chased a bird across the street. The bird flitted up to telephone wires. The dog barked. A car flipped its high beams, honked, slammed brakes. The dog put out its right front paw, waved, swallowed tires. The car dropped into third and searched for night while Nina and I, half-dressed, ran down the stairs and into the street. I rolled the dying animal into the gutter. The dog wheezed like an air conditioner. Nina said she couldn't stand to look at the animal; she loved it too much. If that were true, I said, you wouldn't have left the door open all night. She pleaded with me not to put my guilt trip on her. Nina adored the terms of popular psychology, spat them out like bubbles. She pressed her face into the still-wet crotch of the animal, into its wine-colored rib cage. She cried. Not for the dog but for her own desolation she cried. Man to man I shook its paw, said good-bye, crossed its legs. An hour later the driver of a white van unlocked the door of the cage and threw Nina's dog into the back like a rug.

Run back, I said, and jump. Nina was light. It was conceivable to me the wind would simply pick her up, carry her across the river, and deposit her neatly in the limbs of one of the trees on my side of the river. The dichotomy bothered me: her side, my side. It suggested two people, married, turned away from each other, sleeping. I'm afraid, she said. Don't be, I said. Basically, she said, at heart, I'm a coward. Basically, I said, so is everybody. I can't do it, she said, I can't, I can't. She sat down and held her head in her hands, thought about things. She punched the ground.

If, momentarily, she was inaccessible, her clothes were not. I undid the knots in her backpack, folded back the flap. I squeezed her clothes into a ball, smelled them, breathed in their musty odor, spilled them across the ground. The moon faded and descended slowly. Falling, but in control, the moon wrapped itself in the curtain of night. The moon retreated into the bottom of the sky. What are you doing? she asked. Worry was embedded in her voice like gallstones. I said nothing and tied cloth into cloth, turned jeans into outstretched arms, knotted her clothes into a rope. Her fat woolen socks. Her patched pairs of jeans with their corroded zippers. Her turquoise sweatshirt, inside out.

Holding on to my end of the clothesline, I threw the other end across the river to Nina. Catch, I called, and the clothes nosed through the night like an eel. She caught her clothes. A line tight as wire stretched between us. Hold on, I said. Now what? she said. Hold on tight and swing across, I said. You're brilliant, she said. I was brilliant. The moon wasn't brilliant. Not even close. Clouds drifted together, threatening rain.

Nina tugged on her end of the clothesline. Just jump? she asked. Yes, I said, hold on tight and jump. I can't, she said. Swing across, I said. I pulled on my end. Don't, she said. She tiptoed to the edge, sized up the river. Are you holding on? I asked. Yes, she said. Tight? Yes. I yanked the clothesline like a bed sheet.

At first I thought she'd make it. She swung through the air like a wrecking ball. She clung to her clothes, screamed, kicked her feet. With two clenched hands I held tight. She was only a few feet away from me, on the upswing, when she lost her grip. The clothes slipped through her hands and she plopped backwards into the river like an enormous fish. Nina, I called. She was gone.

The river sucked her up, sent her downstream, eddied and swirled. She sought the surface, coughed. She cried for help. Like a buoy she bobbed above water. Like a suitcase she sank to the bottom. Virginia Woolf placed a good-sized rock in her coat pocket to make sure. Nina struggled for survival: one moment, alive, determined, searching; the next, hidden, drowned, dead.

I ran toward her, in bare feet, downstream, away from the moon. I hurdled bushes and picked up speed. I dove. Headfirst I dove. I hit the soft muddy bottom of the river, jetted to the surface. I spotted her, swam toward her in a furious Australian crawl, wrapped one arm around her waist. She weighed a ton. With my free arm I dog-paddled toward the bank. The river splashed foam at us and carried us downstream while the moon diminished to a pale empty disc and the bank receded a couple hundred yards every time I reached for it so that I had a fairly strong sense of doing battle with nature. I won. I swam through the current, lunged and thrashed my way across it, then clawed at roots, dug my fingernails into dirt. I pulled her to me. I held on to her, crawled out of the river, dragged her onto the soft slime at the edge.

I lay down on top of her unconscious body and breathed into her pale paper lips. I breathed into her mouth like the wind. I pressed my wetness to her wetness like rags. I pounded on her chest, wanted to know if anyone was home. The bottom of the moon touched the earth at the end of the meadow. I rubbed her neck, tore open her shirt. My feet chipped at pebbles, sank into mud. Cold coursed through my body like wet wires. I thumped her chest like applause. Only the top edge of the moon was still visible. Her legs shook, kicked at the ground. I kissed and kissed and kissed. I licked her teeth, the back of her tongue. I bit her lips like hard candy till they bled. Breathe. Water sprayed out of her mouth like a geyser. She coughed. She puked. Nina breathed.

The moon fell like a bomb.

The Sixties

After Leonard Michaels's
"In the Fifties"

The sixties—which, as everybody knows, began in 1963 and ended in 1974—happened, like a sitcom, in the middle of my living room.

I was student-body president of one of the first desegrated elementary schools in California, and when the BBC came to interview me, I spoke so passionately that they had to stop the film because the cameraman was crying.

By the end of seventh grade it was a profound social embarrassment if you hadn't "gotten married," which meant lost your virginity.

The third-floor roof of our high school overlooked the pool in the middle of the courtyard. People who were tripping would jump off the top of the roof into the pool on Saturday nights. Occasionally the pool would have been drained. If someone dove into the empty pool, it was called a "header."

Yvonne, who wore miniskirts and leather jackets and was by far the school's best girl swimmer, drowned when she tried to swim from Lido Isle all the way out to Catalina immediately after a huge lunch of hash brownies.

A married couple who worked for the McGovern campaign, Janice and Michael, came down from Seattle and stayed in our house from the California primary until the general election. I had such a bad crush on Janice that, on the night of Nixon's landslide, I disconnected the car radio so she'd still be in a good enough mood to come with me as I took old people around to the polls until closing.

I wrote so many satires about capital punishment for the high school newspaper that students who didn't read carefully started calling me "The Beheader."

I heard a rumor that Smith-Corona also made munitions and immediately switched to Olivetti.

As the editor of the *Observer*, the newspaper of the California Democratic Council, my father was at times caught in the middle between opponents and defenders of the Vietnam War. He finally ran a cartoon that showed LBJ surfing off the coast of Cambodia, which made the point about American imperialism. The caption my father wrote was "Up Surf." He was fired within the month, not because of the content of the cartoon but because he didn't know the idiom.

The majority of my nieces and nephews on both sides of my family have first names that are either colors, animals, or trees, or some combination of colors, animals, or trees.

Freshman year of high school we all had to take World Geography, and the first day of class we all had to come up on stage and tell "Glen" what kind of animal we were, then portray this animal for a few seconds. The entire semester there was no mention of anything even remotely related to world geography.

The ecology club held a massive demonstration and littered the courtyard with so many placards that for once I abandoned my capital-punishment theme and wrote a satire about the event. The ecology club retaliated by toilet-papering my house.

My cousin had a phrase, "Tain't no big thang." No one knew where he got it, whether or when it was meant sincerely or ironically, but he said it in response to almost every possible development.

Just before graduating college, he and his girlfriend were arrested for possession of a thousand tabs of acid. His girlfriend told the cops she was going to use them to decorate a Christmas tree. "In June?" one cop asked. "Tain't no big thang," my cousin said.

For sociology class I interviewed sixteen different cliques in our high school and found that precisely three-quarters of the groups made "insider/outcast" distinctions not on the basis of money, appearance, academics, after-school job, or sports. Precisely three-quarters of the groups made "insider/outcast" distinctions on the basis of what kind of drugs you used.

In an article in *Newsweek*, our high school was reported to have the highest drug use per capita of any high school in the United States, and people threw parties for a month straight to protect our number-one ranking.

A friend of my sister's had a life-threatening case of colitis and traveled all over India, looking for a holistic cure, and finally settled for Transcendental Meditation, which seemed to do the trick. Now, if you ask her if she wants to do almost anything, she'll say, "Gotta have time to smell the roses," which is, of course, just another version of "Tain't no big thang."

My sister and her best friend had a bitter fight, from which the relationship never fully recovered, over who was the cutest Monkee, Davy or Mickey.

I broke up with my girlfriend when one day she decided she couldn't stand it any longer and went ahead and shaved her legs.

A friend of my father's lived less than a block from where the Symbionese Liberation Army was being busted on live TV, so we all hurried over to this friend's house, with one eye on the television and the other eye out the window. "It's so real I feel like I can almost smell the smoke," someone said. "You *can* smell the smoke," my father said. The SLA was burning to death and smoke was pouring in an open window.

In the fall of 1974 I left Los Angeles to go to college in Providence, Rhode Island, which I imagined as, quite literally, Providence—a heavenly city populated by seraphic souls. I imagined Rhode Island as an actual island, the exotic edge of the eastern coast. And I saw Brown as enclosed, paradisal space in which strong boys played rugby on fields of snow and then perused Ruskin by gas lamps in marble libraries too old to close; and girls, with thick black hair, good bodies, and great minds, talked about Turgenev at breakfast. The first month of my first semester, black students occupied the administration building and demanded increases in black student enrollment and financial aid. These seemed to me laudable goals, so I went over to become part of the picket line outside the administration building and marched in a circle, chanting, for a few minutes, but the whole event seemed like a really weak imitation of all the demonstrations I'd been going to since I was six years old, and I wanted to get away from groups and the West Coast and my former milieu for a while. A few people from my dormitory hall were tossing around a Frisbee on the back side of the green, and I left the picket line to go join them. That, for me, was the end of the sixties.

The

Sheer

Joy

of

Amoral

Creation

Walter tried hard, he tried very hard indeed, to imagine what that night was like for his mother and father, since the evidence was so strong it had been a night tinged with not a little romance. And yet, although he perceived himself as the possessor of a potentially bold imagination, he experienced considerable difficulty when he tried to visualize the embrace that brought about his birth. He had never seen them so much as kiss except at a California Democratic Council New Year's Eve fund-raiser, 1966, when his father drank so many vodkas and soda without the soda that at midnight he threw confetti at the clock and said, "Pull me in, sweet, pull me in," locking his lips with hers and rubbing the back of her head until 1967 held very definite promise of things to come. Walt's childhood bedroom had been directly below theirs, but even when he stood on top of his desk and listened to the open air vent for the creak of the bed, he never heard anything more than the sound of cool air whipping through a dark grate. They never held hands, Walter thought, they never touched.

Three weeks before she died, Walter's mother slipped off the commode and her gown caught on the aluminum side bar, which left Walter to look at her naked from the navel down. It was not a pretty sight—skinny white legs stretched into a V and vibrating until he lifted her off the floor. But surely she was not always as desiccated as this. One winter Walter and his mother swam every week at an indoor pool, and every week an old lady wearing blue goggles and fins asked if they were brother and sister. Another winter she got tired of walking around City Hall with wet feet and bought a pair of black leather boots with two-inch heels; so many of her fellow reporters asked what she was doing tonight that she threw the boots in the closet and never wore them again. Walter showed a color photograph of his mother to Nina, who said, "I didn't think she'd be so good-looking." Although Walter didn't think his mother was so good-looking, he wondered why Nina didn't think she would be. In the photograph, taken at a party in celebration of her return from the hospital, his mother looked much more beautiful than she ever had before: thin, delicate, admirably self-contained.

On the anniversary of his mother's death, Walter's father visited Walter and Nina in Providence. While Nina slept wrapped in wool pajamas and knee socks next to an electric heater burning orange coils on the floor near the head of the bed, Walter walked around in the snow with his father, who said, "I've been more active this year with Renée than I'd been the previous twenty-five with your mother, and I don't mean once a night. I mean two or three times a night most every night of the week and then again in the morning." Walter slipped on ice and his father threw a snowball at a tree and missed and said (quoting Sartre, for he was always quoting Sartre), "I like the horse I ride, I like my freedom." Walter liked neither horses nor freedom, since the only horse he had ever ridden shook him out of the saddle, very nearly stomping him to death, and freedom—distance from Nina—seemed exciting for about six hours until he had convinced himself she was a saint.

When Walter's mother died, his father decided to sell the house, but a year before she died she had divorced him and altered her will so that Walter and Ellen would get everything she owned, which included her half of the house. Walter said, "Sell it." Ellen, who always loved things (a glass case of Japanese dolls her uncle had brought back from the war and given her, a rocking chair which the antique dealer said could not be later than 1835 and might be as early as late eighteenth century, although it did have new runners) and who later insisted upon saving every article of clothing her mother had ever worn, couldn't part easily with all of the history which was the house she had grown up in. She sat on the living-room floor and dusted off first editions, placing them in a separate pile, and packed books into boxes while Walter walked around the den and told his father not to stop and read every article about Cesar Chavez his mother had ever written. Walter kept wondering aloud what it was like to finally be free of your lifelong antagonist until his father said, "There were periods, Walt, there were long stretches of time that I thought would never end, when I failed with your mother." That was what Walter wanted to hear, and now that he had heard it, he didn't want to hear anymore, but his father thought he needed to explain, and after a few minutes his confession became so clear that he cried into the large wastebasket, using his wife's old articles as so many hankies.

Walter understood how his father might have lost his desire for his wife, since Walter remembered her as having short black hair, blue veins popping through white skin, and boyish hips. He knew she could not possibly have had red eyes and yet—on the basis of one photograph, which was shot with too much flash—he remembered her eyes as the frenzied red eyes of an angry mouse. He knew she'd been five foot seven, but he was unable to remember her other than as an impossibly light, frail being whose bones were collapsing and whose flesh was falling off as she slowly became less visible and then vanished. He imagined her in bed with her back against the headboard, smoking a cigarette and editing a book about the condition of farm workers in Salinas. And then Walter imagined she would untie her bathrobe and lift her nightgown and pull back the covers and, as she had done all day, advise her husband on what to do. He could pretend to sleep and snore for only so long. He would try once and try again, he would fail and say, "I'm so sorry, sweet," and cry into her arms until she had fallen asleep.

Walter's mother often used to reminisce about how, until he was born, she and his father and Ellen lived in a nice little duplex in Hollywood on Orange Drive. Walter blamed his birth not only for the beginning of all his own troubles but for the downfall of his family as well, since shortly after his emergence they left Hollywood for a ranch house in Griffith Park. He had never seen his original neighborhood except in photographs. Once, when he and Nina traveled cross-country partly in order for him to scrutinize the apartment he had heard so much about, they could find no such address (he must have copied it down wrong), and his main impression of Orange Drive was of a kind of quiet tunnel between the prostitutes on Sunset Boulevard and the massage parlors on Melrose, so he was forced to imagine what it had been like, and he couldn't. It wasn't in him. He tried but he simply couldn't.

Shortly after his mother's death, Walter hoped to find somewhere in all her papers at least one thing that contradicted the completely stoical persona she'd presented to the world, since he didn't believe in heroes or heroines. Her last will and testament had a handwritten note stapled to the back of it:

> In the event of my death, I would like to have my body cremated and the ashes disposed of in the simplest way possible. My first choice would have been to donate my heart, kidneys, and cornea for transplants. However, it is not possible to donate the organs of someone with cancer. I realize that cremation is not in accordance with Jewish law, but I think it is the most sensible method of disposing of a lifeless body. Although I do not want a religious memorial service, I hope it is helpful to family and friends to have an informal gathering of people, so that each may draw strength from one another. I leave this world without regrets or bitterness of any kind. I have had a good life. May the future be kind to each of you. Shalom.

To Walter, there was something unnatural, almost spooky about his mother's matter-of-fact tone, especially since the disease's recent, final recurrence was several years after doctors had said it had gone into complete remission. She had apparently started a journal a few months before dying but never got back to it after this first, formal entry:

> Of one thing I'm sure: I don't want to live if I can't function, make decisions for myself, and take care of

myself. I hope that if I reach that point I'll have the courage to take my life. I feel very strongly that life is a very precious gift and that one should always choose life, but to me life is being able to function. Maybe I'll be able to express this better and more clearly as time goes on.

Walter was quite cowardly when it came to his own mortality, and if he admired his mother's sentiments, he also had trouble truly understanding them. He wanted to find one thing about his mother he understood, instinctively. She had an entire broken suitcase full of scraps of papers on which her employers had paid her professional compliments: "I enjoyed this issue very much." "The layout really had movement." "Your patience, concern, and insight are most noteworthy." "You are, without the slightest reservations as to character, ability, or personality, the finest newspaperwoman I have ever had the pleasure of working with." Walter did essentially the same thing with his professors' comments as his mother did with her bosses' little bouquets of praise, but he had been impressed with his mother all his life; he was hoping to come across a piece of paper that attacked his heart.

All the condolences were only more journalistic encomia: "She always brightened the city room with her sparkle and excellent ideas." "It was a delight and privilege to work with her all these years." ". . . my deep respect for her professionalism, intelligence, and capability . . ." These people didn't seem, to Walter, to be talking about a real person; they were describing some cardboard cutout of Lillian Hellman. Walter needed to get past the cartoon and clichés to someone who wasn't a ghost, who was physical. "She was a talented professional, a remarkable woman."

Save for the first paragraph, Walter's mother had written

even her own obituary, which recounted her jobs with more than a dozen progressive newspapers, magazines, and organizations: coordinator of public information, researcher, writer, correspondent, editor, managing editor. The final sentence of the obituary read: "Mrs. Jaffe requested that friends make a memorial gift to the United Farm Workers." Walter couldn't help but laugh a little; maybe there really was nothing about his mother that wasn't public-minded and altruistic. About twenty copies of the obituary had been photocopied (by his father, Walter supposed), and Walter threw them up in the air. A tiny piece of completely yellowed paper slid out from the obituaries as they fluttered back down. It was a poem—"I Need Not Tell You Why," by Thomas Emmet Moore—that looked like it must have been cut out of her college textbook:

> I did not dream you could forget,
>   I could not know that love may die;
> I only know my eyes are wet,
>   And that I need not tell you why!
>
> I need not tell you why, dear heart—
>   Your cold lips would deny;
> But well I know that love is fled,
>   I need not tell you why!
>
> You smile, and kiss me, and I hear
>   You say your love is strong and true
> As when you wooed me; yesteryear,
>   To leave my world and follow you!
>
> You say my hair is as the foam
>   That crowns a cup of amber wine;
> But though you've called me to your home,
>   Your love, dear heart, is now not mine!
>
> Nay, do not fold me to your breast,
>   You well should know you give but pain;

> For aching hearts there is no rest
> Till love hath healed their wounds again!

Although he was an English major, Walter had never heard of Thomas Emmet Moore, so he went into the den, opened the encyclopedia, and discovered that Moore was an Irish poet who was born in 1779 and died in 1852. He was born and he died and he lived and he loved and he lost and he wrote at least one really bad poem. Which didn't matter, because the poem was a revelation to Walter. Never had he considered even the possibility that his mother could harbor such helpless, primitive, irrational feelings; never had he considered the possibility that it would be permissible for himself to feel such feelings, since so much of dinner table conversation had centered around the nuances of political and journalistic propriety. Walter wished and wished and wished that on the night of his conception (and on subsequent days and nights) his mother and father had communicated to each other (and thus to him) not that the body was moral, which it wasn't, but that it was mortal, only mortal, and that the act of love wasn't one more good deed but a riot of feelings, for if they had, if they only had, he would have become (he was virtually certain of it) a more imaginative person than he was now.

Father's Day

My father comes up from Los Angeles to visit for the weekend, and my Father's Day present, six days late, is box seats to a Mariners game. I'm new to Seattle and this is the first time I've been inside the Kingdome, which, with its navy blues and fern greens, looks to me like an aquarium for tropical fish. The Kingdome reminds my father of "dinner theater" and he wants to know where's John Barrymore. My father turns seventy-nine next month; when he's eighty, he wants to quit his part-time job and drive a Winnebago cross-country, then fly to Wimbledon to eat strawberries and cream.

His second cousin was an actor on the Yiddish stage and later, as Captain Dreyfus in *The Life of Emile Zola*, won an Academy Award for best supporting actor. A moderately well-known mime is supposedly a relative. When Danny Kaye was performing at the Hollywood Bowl in the mid-fifties, he asked everyone from P.S. 149 to stand and half a dozen people did. Then he asked anyone who remembered the P.S. 149 fight song to sing it. Only my father stayed standing. "Sit down, Leonard," my father remembers my mother saying. "Please. This is so embarrassing." There is something in me, in my father's side of the family, that always seems to be looking around for the possibility of applause.

The sixth-place Mariners are playing the last-place Tigers on Barbecue Apron Night. Watching batting practice, we fold and unfold our plastic Mariners barbecue aprons, which smell disconcertingly like formaldehyde, and we run through all the baseball anecdotes he's told me all my life, only this time—because I press him—he tells each story without embellishment. He'd always said that he played semi-pro baseball, and I had images of him sliding across glass-strewn sandlots to earn food money; it was only guys from another neighborhood occasionally paying him ten bucks to play on their pickup team and throw his "dinky curve." He used to say that he was team captain for an Army all-star baseball team that toured overseas, and as a kid I convinced myself that he spent 1943 in Okinawa, hitting fungoes to Ted Williams and Joe DiMaggio. He was only traveling secretary, the most prominent player on the team was a Detroit Tiger named Pat Mullins, and it was fast-pitch softball Stateside.

My father still looks somewhat, and used to look almost exactly, like Leo Durocher. Once, when we were living in Los Angeles, the garbageman supposedly shook my father's hand and said, "Sorry to hear about your marriage, Mr. Durocher." Durocher had been recently divorced from the actress Laraine Day; the garbageman was being sympathetic in a male mode—so went the story. And for some reason I always thought my father stood atop the trash in the back of the truck, hefted garbage cans with one hand, and cursed The Fishbowl Which Is Hollywood, whereas in actuality my father immediately told my mother about impersonating Leo Durocher, she cautioned him against stringing along the innocent garbage collector, and my father chased down the truck to explain and make amends.

Before the game, there's a "Peace Run" around the field—some sort of marathon-for-a-cause which I don't quite catch because the P.A. system sounds like it's being filtered through a car wash—then the umpires stroll onto the Astroturf, but since this is Seattle, they aren't booed even a little, which disappoints my father. In 1940 he was the star student at a Florida umpire school run by Bill McGowan, who said my father could become "another Dolly Stark"—i.e., a Jewish umpire—but before reporting to Class D ball my father begged off, citing his poor night vision. He wound up umping Brooklyn College–Seton Hall games and once got whacked over the head with a malacca walking stick when he called someone's favorite son out at home with two on, two out, the score tied, and the light, I guess, failing. My father's favorite Bill McGowan story concerns the time McGowan, a former amateur boxer, grew weary of Babe Ruth's grousing and, during the intermission of a doubleheader, challenged the Babe to a fight. The Babe backed down. I hope this much is clear: the hero of my father's stories is always someone else. It's never him.

The Mariners score three in the first. Keith Moreland looks painfully uncomfortable at third for the Tigers. Ken Griffey, Jr., makes a nice catch in the fifth. But we're Dodger fans and so the game is largely devoid of any real drama for either of us—as my father says, "like watching a movie when you don't care what happens to the characters." My father grew up playing stickball in Brownsville; every few innings, he and his friends would run over to a pool hall to check the Dodger scores as they came in over the ticker tape and were posted on a blackboard outside. Zack Wheat. Dazzy Vance. Wilbert Robinson. He moved to Los Angeles in 1946, and apparently, while my mother was suffering blackout spells during a late-summer heat wave, he flew back to New York, ostensibly to attend his father's eighty-fifth birthday party but, more particularly, to attend the 1955 World Series and, even more particularly, watch the Dodgers finally beat the Yankees and, more particularly still, watch Jackie Robinson steal home under Yogi Berra's tag. I have my father's pictures of press row at Yankee Stadium; look at the snap-brim hats.

In our family mythology this flight of my father's has always been painted in the darkest of colors, and yet when I was a child I would look first thing each morning at the box scores and cry ickily into my cereal if the Dodgers had lost. I remember defacing my Ron Perranoski baseball card when he failed to hold a huge lead going into the ninth, pushing over my grandfather's television set when it broadcast Dodger right fielder Ron Fairly's transformation of an obvious out into a home run over the low right-field wall at Dodger Stadium, engaging in a weird sort of mock-Ophelia thing at the beach after the fiasco of the 1966 Series against the Orioles. What was this obsession we had with the Dodgers? "For me, it comes out this way," my father will write me the week after this Father's Day visit. "I wanted the Dodgers to compensate for some of the unrealized goals in my career. What do they call that in Freudian terms—transfer, is that right? If I wasn't winning my battle to succeed in newspapering, union organizing, or whatever I turned to in my wholly unplanned, anarchic life, then my surrogates—the nine boys in blue—could win against the Giants, Pirates, et al. Farfetched? Maybe so. But I think it has some validity. In my case. Not in yours."

Oh, no; not in mine; never in mine.

Although the Kingdome has, even by ballpark standards, notoriously bad food, we decide to stand in line at the concession, anyway, not because we're so hungry but because we need something to do while a wave is going around the stadium. My father and I both get a hot dog and a beer, and we share a bag of peanuts—which comes to an amazing amount of money, for a meal my father says has the nutritional quotient of a resin bag. To my father's astonishment, I top off this indigestible dinner with a chocolate malt, which looks almost purple and tastes as bitter as coffee. We return to our seats. The wave's still rising and falling, or maybe it's a new wave.

Sixty years ago he was a sports stringer for the *New York Journal-American*; now he's sports editor and photographer for a suburban weekly, for which he covers the Little League, Pony League, Colt League, men's fast-pitch softball, and women's softball. Three days before he came up to visit, he was trying to take a photograph of a Little Leaguer stealing third base and the catcher's throw hit my father in the ankle, breaking three blood vessels. He's proud of his bruised ankle and he keeps showing it to me, enacting the scene, saying with a sportswriter's mix of hyperbole and mixed metaphor: "It blew up like an egg."

He always sends me the column he writes for his tennis-club newsletter. This is by far my favorite lead: "A hundred members and guests attended the annual Tennis Club meeting and, to coin a forgettable phrase, a helluva time was had by all and sundry. (Especially Sundry, who seemed to be having the time of his life.)" When I'm in certain moods, this Borscht Belt humor can completely convulse me.

It's the seventh-inning stretch, with the Mariners up 3–1, and just as in order to express some sort of vague rebellion we didn't stand up during the National Anthem, now during the seventh-inning stretch we don't stretch, although I can't help but watch the "full-matrix scoreboard," which is flashing images of fans stretching. All fifteen thousand fans in the Kingdome are watching the scoreboard, waiting to find out whether they're beautiful enough to be broadcast, since virtually without exception the images are Pacific Northwest–perfect: sleeping babies wearing Mariners caps, energetic grandparents, couples kissing. The moment people are shown they point at the screen, then they point at themselves pointing at themselves on the screen, then everyone points at them pointing at themselves pointing at themselves on the screen. I continue looking at the scoreboard, wanting my chance to point at myself pointing at myself on the screen, and then I look over at my father, who hasn't been watching the screen at all. He always keeps score, and he's tidying up his scorecard. He's no longer looking to be lifted onto an empyrean matrix; he just wants to eat strawberries and cream at Wimbledon the summer of his eightieth birthday. "Presley, Martinez, and Vizquel coming up for the Mariners," he says, and we go to the bottom of the seventh.

Junk

I bounced up and down in the backseat of the car in order to obstruct my father's vision out the rearview mirror. He told me to sit down, but I shook my head and looked into the mirror at my face, so he pulled off the highway into a rest stop, unrolled his window, carefully examined his whiskers, and rubbed his cheeks and chin in the side-view mirror. I turned and whispered into Ellen's ear, then rattled the outstretched newspaper behind which my mother hid. When I slid up to the edge of the seat and tugged at the sleeve of my father's white shirt, he unbuckled his seat belt and turned around to face me.

"Dad?" I said, cupping my hand over my mouth, sinking back into the seat.

"What?"

"What did I do?"

"I need to be able to see out the rearview mirror," he said. "I have to know what's happening behind me. A clear rearview mirror prevents accidents, Walt. You know that. You wouldn't want to cause an accident, would you?"

"I was only—"

"Walt," my mother said.

We got back on the road again. I leaned forward and stretched my hand out the window, letting the wind drag my arm back. The street was lined with eucalyptus trees swaying in the wind, and the sun gleamed through the blue holes between the branches of the trees. I got up on my haunches and stuck my head out the window until I was almost sitting on the windowsill. I asked my father if we were near my grandfather's house yet, but he didn't hear me and cupped his hand over his right ear. My mother yanked me down into the seat, rolling up the window and snapping the seat belt around my waist.

"I didn't hear you," my father said.

"Sorry."

"What did you say? I didn't hear you."

"Nothing."

"What did you say?"

"Are we almost there?"

"Is that what you said?"

"Yes."

"You almost fell out the window," my mother said.

"Well, are we?"

"A few more hours."

"Why does it take so long?" I asked, squirming away from my mother.

"It just does. You'll have to be patient, Walt."

"What are we going to do when we get there?"

"Talk with them."

"About what?"

"About how your father is not going to take over Poppa's store for him," my mother said.

It was late at night and there were no other cars on the street when we edged into the garage of my grandparents' square one-story house. The back door was open. They had already gone to bed. The wooden floor creaked; antique chests and cabinets were covered with dainty decorations. I was cold and I shivered, so I went into the room Ellen had claimed.

"You're not going to sleep in here," she said.

"Why not? I don't want to sleep with Dad."

"Boys and girls aren't supposed to sleep in the same bed."

"But we're only—"

"Still."

"Really?"

Ellen giggled and put her head under the pillow. "Of course."

While my parents washed up, I walked around the house on my tiptoes, in my socks. In the totally dark dining room, I walked by grabbing for the backs of chairs and the corners of walls, like a blind man. I bumped into something large. Frantically thumping the walls, I found the light switch. I looked up at the gold face of a grandfather clock, which had black hands set to the wrong time. Three long cylinders hung from the clock's diaphragm. A pendulum swung in a jerky rhythm.

I turned out the light. The room seemed to descend, leaving me stranded in air, as if I'd slipped off a whirling centrifuge. I stretched my arms out ahead of me to feel the doors and walls, hurried into the den, and slipped under the icy covers. My father was already asleep in the middle of the double bed.

"Get up," Ellen whispered, waking me in the morning.

I tried to pull the covers over my head, but she yanked the top blanket out of my hands.

"Get up. Poppa's leaving for the shop."

"Tell him to wait a minute."

"He can't."

I stumbled into the kitchen, and my father seemed to need to cue my response—wrapping his arms around himself and pointing at my grandparents. I hugged my grandfather, his scraggly whiskers grazing my cheeks. My grandmother's strands of white hair wound into my mouth as I kissed her powdered cheeks.

"I'll see you at the shop, young man," my grandfather said to me. "I'm late."

Hand-lettered signs hung from the wooden pillars of my grandfather's cavernous store: COME BROWSE TO YOUR HEART'S DELIGHT. FRESH MERCHANDISE DAILY. ALL SALES FINAL. PLEASE LEAVE ALL SHOPPING BAGS AT CHECK STAND. NO EXCHANGES, NO REFUNDS. And every item—every couch without cushions, every dirt-ringed deodorizer and humidifier, every box of mismatched train tracks, every purse with a broken clasp, every shopping cart of doilies and linen and welcome mats, every sleeveless record, every mattress with what my grandfather called "give," every radio and television with fuzzy reception, every tarnished gold medal, every incomplete set of encyclopedias, every faded daguerreotype, every stove missing burners and knobs, every filmy wine and beer and water glass, every worn-out wallet, every piano with chipped keys, every suitcase that didn't shut all the way, every wig on a mannequin head, every outdated hi-fi—every item in the entire building carried the label: "This article sold *as is* and with *all faults.*"

While a few customers were moseying around the back of the store, my grandfather sat up on his stool at the register, turned to me, and asked how would I like to have the big clock he had at home. I said it was broken. He said he could fix it. I asked if the pendulum would swing right. He said it would. He said the clock would gong, too, but he couldn't give me the clock unless I agreed to mind the store when I was old enough. I refused and told him he could take back his broken clock. He said that I'd already agreed to accept the clock and that, if I was a man and not a boy, I would not back out of the deal. I was a boy and cried.

"The clock's mine," I said. "You gave it to me."

"I gave you the store, too. You must take it."

"I don't want it."

"You must, Walt."

"Everything here is so old and broken."

"So is the clock."

"But you said you could fix it."

"I can fix everything else here, too. You can learn how from me."

"I only want the clock."

"I've already given you the clock. I can't take it back. But you must also take over the store. That was the agreement."

"I don't want the clock anymore."

"It's yours."

"No."

"I've already given it to you," he said and got up to go talk to the customers. Nothing in the whole huge place was new or shiny. Everything had dirt on it, in it, buried deep in its bones. The concrete floor was badly cracked and covered in soot. Dust everywhere made me sneeze.

"I don't want it. I don't want this dumb store."

"It's yours," he said. "Forever. I want to give it to you."

With him calling after me, I ran screaming out of my grandfather's shop onto the busy avenue.

When my family returned to our house, my sister and I spent days researching how best to spend the twenty-dollar bills my grandfather had tucked into our suitcases. My father told me to get a camera. I really didn't want a camera but couldn't think of anything else I wanted. He took me downtown to a camera shop, where I pointed to a display model and said I wanted that one. My father stepped up from behind and said, "That's way too expensive, Walt." He pointed to another camera, which cost just under twenty dollars. The sales tax broke me, and my father paid the difference.

As we drove home, I said to my father, "I didn't even want that one."

"It's a good simple little Brownie. You can take nice pictures with it. Of your mother. Of Ellen. Even of me, if you want."

"But this isn't the one I wanted." I fumbled with the latch to the camera case.

"Don't complain, Walt. It's what you could afford."

My father said that in a few weeks my grandparents were coming to stay at our house until they found an apartment near us. Lying flat on the dining-room table was the letter my grandfather had written my father. His handwriting looked a lot like mine, except his loops skidded whereas mine swept. He had a buyer for the shop. He wanted to retire. He asked if they could stay at our house for a short time until they found an apartment nearby.

"Hi, Poppa," I said as he walked off the plane, sliding his suitcase along the ground. I hugged him, picked up the suitcase, put it down, kissed my grandmother (who smelled like blintzes), picked up the suitcase, and we started walking toward our car.

"How was the flight?" my father asked.

Grabbing his cane before it fell to the floor, my grandfather asked how I had spent my twenty dollars.

"On a camera" I said. "Wanna see it when we get home?"

"What can you do with a camera?"

"Take pictures."

"Of what?"

"All kinds of things."

"*Acch*," he said and turned to my sister. "Did you spend your money yet, Ellen?"

"Yes, I bought a watch."

"A watch? Can you tell time?"

Everyone laughed.

"Of course, Poppa. Even Walt can tell time." Ellen reached over to jab me in the stomach. "It's twenty of three."

My grandfather smiled and put his arm around my shoulder. "Take a lesson from your sister. She bought something useful—practically a necessity. And you go and buy a luxury item like a camera."

.   .   .

My grandfather pressed the intercom buzzer. Through a first-floor window I watched the manager in his apartment talk to my grandparents over the intercom. The television picture in back of the manager kept jumping.

"Got any pets?" the manager asked over the intercom.

My grandmother shook her head. Then she realized she couldn't be seen and entered an emphatic "No" into the intercom. A buzzer beeped. The stucco was painted pink; ice plant bloomed in the courtyard; a little wading pool was being drained. My grandfather walked around his empty future apartment. "I'm ready to relax," he said. "That damn shop gave me enough trouble. You'll be all right here, won't you, Muriel? Close to them, no worries. You'll like it here." My grandmother was looking out the window at the garden.

The unwieldy furniture from their old house had been crammed like museum pieces into their new apartment. My grandfather was sitting on the couch. A radio somewhere was playing big-band music. The newspaper was turned to the obituaries. He had a bourbon in his hand at eleven o'clock on a Sunday morning. I held my camera in its case.

"Look, Poppa. I brought my camera. Can I take a picture of you?"

"Give me that thing."

"Oh, come on, Dad," my father said. "Let Walt take just one picture. That's all he talked about at breakfast."

"No," my grandfather said. "I don't want those flashballs going off in my face."

"I don't need any flash. There's lots of light."

He tightened the belt on his bathrobe while I slipped out of the room into the hallway to take the camera out of its case. My father shook his head when he saw me adjusting the dials. My grandfather saw him shake his head.

"Wait," my grandfather said. "Don't."

He flicked his cane and toppled the camera out of my hands just as I was pressing the button. The camera bounced off the wooden coffee table and landed on the carpet.

I used up the rest of the roll taking pictures of my father sleeping; of my mother and sister looking into the flame of a candle; of my grandmother, her white strands of hair curling into her mouth; and one of myself in the mirror. The next Saturday I went to the camera shop with my father, who paid the salesman for the pictures. When my grandfather dislodged the camera from my hands, he must have jarred the roll of film because most of the photographs were fuzzy, as if I had a shaky hand. All these years I've kept only the most distorted print from the entire roll. It doesn't have the silky, glossy finish of the other prints. The neat white border is demolished. The photo runs all the way to the edge. Two negative images form a double exposure. Poppa: black face, black shirt, white pants, arm raised, cane grasped in his hard right hand. His face is out of focus. The background of the picture is clear: the grandfather clock's white hands, face, and cylinders glistening. Overlapping is the negative of me: white hair, black face, the bathroom light exploding off the mirror into my eyes.

Oaxaca

Every time the house creaked it was, to Walter, his mother falling out of bed in her sleep; every phone call was she asking him for help on the new line she'd had installed in his room; every rush of the wind was her last wheezing breath. But every footfall, every swing of a gate, every approaching voice, every closed car door was Leanne. He'd grown up with her—he'd known her all his life—but only this summer had he started to think about her when she wasn't there. Once in a while she'd be driving around town and decide to climb over the fence, race across the back lawn, and knock on the door to Walter's bedroom. She would bring over bottles of beer for them to share as they sat and talked, although she would usually drink most of the beer, since Walter had never drunk much before. She would also bring recent records she had heard on the radio and play them on Walter's stereo over and over until she knew all the words by heart and Walter could discern a phrase here and there if he listened closely. Music didn't mean that much to him.

Then they would dance, but quietly, very quietly, because Walter's mother was always trying to sleep directly upstairs. Walter hadn't danced since he was eleven years old, so Leanne tried to teach him some steps, but he resisted because sometimes he thought she was showing him how to do too many things, that she was trying to teach him how to live, and he didn't like that. He wanted to remember who he had always been: a nervous little boy cowering in the corner. When he most desperately wanted her to be there, she would be in Tahoe for the weekend with her family, and when he was temporarily tired of her, she'd invariably show her face in the glass window of the door to his room. Tonight, just as he was falling asleep, he heard the rap of her knuckle knocking on wood.

Walter turned on the overhead light. He had yet to be seen naked (or, for that matter, kissed) by Leanne, so he put on his bathrobe before opening the door. She was smiling and squinting in the porch light; she was carrying car keys, records, and a six-pack of Dos Equis; she was wearing sandals she'd bought, after lengthy negotiations, in an open-air market in Oaxaca for two dollars and twenty-five cents, short shorts, and a blue swimsuit top still wet from a midnight dip in her parents' pool. It was common knowledge, she would say, that she was "attractive," but Walter couldn't look at her without seeing flaws: bulky gold-rimmed glasses and, behind the lenses, the shallow green eyes of a cat; a thick, throaty neck; a patch of freckles across a high white forehead. And she had a lap. She was the only girl he knew who, when she sat down, quite clearly had a lap.

Leanne turned on the stereo and then the fan, which drowned out the stereo, and she opened the shades, the windows, and the door. She didn't care about breezes or cross breezes or circulation: she just wanted wild white noises next to hot night air. She wanted Walter to stop being a boy, but all he did was say, "We should probably turn it down a little. My mother's trying to get some sleep."

He sat at the foot of the bed and watched her dance slowly around the room, spilling her bottle of beer on the rug, until she stopped and stood over him and said, "Walter, don't you want to dance?"

He danced, but alone and away from her, with his back turned toward her. The record repeated the sentiment that, if he couldn't love her, he didn't want to love nobody, and Walter, given his family history—his parents were in the middle of a trial separation; his sister's engagement to someone at school had just been broken off—distrusted the sentiment. He desired every gorgeous girl who walked past him on the street, but he thought he was uninterested in or incapable of loving any one of them in particular, even Leanne, although perhaps this was because he'd never loved any woman other than his mother, and about her he was feeling fairly ambivalent right now.

Leanne turned down the music a little and said, "I want us to dance together."

Rather than answer, Walter poked his head out the window, felt with his fingertips the damp ground and the dew on the grass, and twisted his neck so he could see massive sycamore trees across the street still and stiff in the windless night.

"I want to dance with *you*," she said.

"You are. You already are."

"But together," she said. "To the same beat and touching."

Walter wheeled toward the window, but Leanne held him by the arm and turned up the music loud as she tugged him toward the center of the room. She tried to teach him a dance in which he lifted his left arm high and bent and held her hand while she twirled around him and twirled back so that the two of them formed a sort of fluid figure eight. But at the finish of each spin he was supposed to swing her back to him to begin again. He was too conscious of his mother upstairs to concentrate on what he was supposed to be doing with Leanne; over and over again she spun away from him and waited to be spun back, only to stay there, lunging, squeezing his hand, at the wrong end of his long left arm.

"Relax, Walter. You're too tight. Relax your arms."

"I am relaxed."

"No you aren't. Let your arms go limp."

"Okay."

"Now loosen up your shoulders. You're still tense."

"No I'm not."

"Now swing me out, and when you feel a little tug at the end of your arm, swing me back with a little wrist action."

"I just swing you right back?"

"Yes, now pull me in."

His arm, vibrating and rigid, was stuck straight out so that no matter how many times Leanne continued to say, "Now swing me right back toward you," he was unable to move a muscle while she stood with one hand on her hip and the other holding his hand, waiting, waiting. When, once too many times, she said, "I'm not going to move until you swing me back," and her posture took on the quality of a pout, Walter, not sure what he was doing other than that what he was doing wasn't because he felt any sudden flush of feeling for her but only to shut her up, pulled Leanne to him with trembling arms. He smelled the beer on her breath, and taking off her glasses, looked at her eyes (which were red from chlorine in her parents' pool), and then he kissed her: the first full kiss of his life. Kissing the freckles on her forehead, he suddenly could imagine himself and Leanne taking off together down to Oaxaca—where Indians carried tiny cages full of brightly colored tropical birds, vendors sold chunks of pineapple on a stick, and bougainvillea dropped pink petals into the fountain in the courtyard and of the hotel. His arms were wrapped around her shoulders; her belt buckle clanked against his. Although at first it sounded like just part of the song, on the second ring Walter could tell the phone was definitely ringing. He looked at the clock. It was one in the morning.

"You must have another admirer," Leanne said.

"It's my mother," Walter said.

"I know," Leanne said. "What would happen if you didn't answer? I mean, wouldn't she just go back to sleep?"

"No," Walter said, "I can't do that. I wish I could, but I can't. That wouldn't be right, no. I mean, how could I do that with a clear conscience?"

Walter got down on his hands and knees to help Leanne search for her other sandal.

The Fourth Wonder of the World

Sylvia had persuaded her family to come to Jackson Hole by describing how, all along the ridges of the Grand Tetons, snow sparkled in the sun. The children had never seen snow before, so now Ellen was taking pictures with Leonard's camera and Walt was bounding like a deer toward the base of the mountain. Shortly after they all started up the trail for the high country, a ranger asked if they had an ice axe.

"An ice axe?" Leonard said.

The ranger, a jolly man with a pipe in his mouth and white skin burned first-degree violet, said, "Yes, high-country trails are still covered with snow."

"Oh," Sylvia said, brushing inadvertently against the ranger's arm, "don't worry. We'll turn back if the trail turns too icy."

She slurped warm water from her canteen to suggest something—she wasn't sure what; that she was no novice backpacker?—but the ranger said, "I'm going to have to ask you folks to stay off the high-country trails until the first of August. In ten days you'll be back in business."

"Ten days!" the children shrieked, and Leonard muttered that the ranger was a fascist.

Ten days was entirely too long to wait, but they were here, after all, and to come this far and then turn around and go back seemed to Sylvia so absurd that she persuaded them to stay until they had seen every view of the valley at least once. Walt and Ellen went out exploring and returned with tales of swans sailing down the Snake River and baby bears eating out of people's hands. Sylvia took pictures of every flower she came across, and whenever she returned from a photographic expedition, she could always count on finding Leonard back at the cabin—sitting in a green-and-white plastic lawn chair and reminding her that roll after color roll of film was not inexpensive and that postcards would be cheaper and just as pretty.

At night they stayed inside the cabin, a small square room with two twin beds and a telephone which was out of order. Leonard told Walt war stories. Ellen squeezed her blackheads in a full-length mirror propped up between the beds. Sylvia wrote postcards to people at work and said, as gently as she could, "Now, Leonard, you know that's not true."

Walt giggled nonstop and Ellen got up every hour or so to sit on a splintered stool and hold her nose in the outhouse because—she told Sylvia—she felt her first period coming on. Leonard snored, and when she finally fell asleep each night, Sylvia slept soundly, but the third night they were there it rained so hard that water streamed through the crack at the base of the front door.

Sylvia, turning to touch Leonard, felt wet wood and

awoke with a howl. Everyone sat up, looking at Sylvia, but she felt like just listening to the rainfall for a while and not saying much. When she was unable to get back to sleep, though, she insisted that they simply pick up and leave in the middle of the night. She was weary of hearing the ranger tell her that by the end of the week they'd be taking pictures of Jackson Lake from the top of the Tetons, weary of waiting for dinner in a long line outside the lodge and chatting with cute young couples so obviously in love. With all the lights in the room on and the radio turned up high and the wind shaking the windows, she packed all their suitcases and marched them through the downpour out to the car.

As Leonard drove south and slightly west on Highway 89, Sylvia wondered what it was she hated so much about the way he'd swerve slightly off the pavement onto gravel or misread a road sign and take a wrong turn. Passing Salt Lake City, Sylvia pointed out to him a warehouse roof painted red, white, and blue and spelling MCCARTHY, since Leonard was always telling her that McCarthy was, more or less, his man. He asked her, even as he was doing it, what she thought of him turning off the freeway and coasting down the embankment to the parking lot across the street from the warehouse.

Leonard got out of the car and did jumping jacks to get his blood circulating. He was always either reading or exercising; didn't he ever just want to take a look around? He slapped his hands loudly over his head. Birds, beautiful, beautiful bluebirds circled above him, but he scared them back to their trees and telephone poles with his flapping. The children awoke.

"Where are we?" Walt asked.

"Idaho," Sylvia said, which sent Walt and Ellen into insane laughter, and they both immediately said: "Idaho; Alaska: I don't know; I'll ask her."

Walt asked, "Where in Idaho?"

"Boise."

"Why did we stop *here?*" Ellen said, imitating almost exactly the tone of voice Sylvia used to indicate bored restlessness.

Sylvia said, "Your father wanted to stretch his legs."

Ellen said she felt cramps coming on and wanted to know where the bathroom was, and Walt asked Sylvia for a quarter to buy licorice from the machines, then asked if he could get her anything.

"No," Sylvia said, "you get what you want."

Leonard stopped stretching his legs to tell Sylvia that they were not in Idaho, but Utah; not in Boise, but Salt Lake. Sylvia was too exhausted to do anything more than nod.

When Leonard saw the posters stuck to the cement walls of the warehouse, he said he wanted to stay for the rally, which he was sure would be starting soon. In a few hours, Sylvia knew Leonard was thinking, thunderous helicopters would be flying overhead and sleek black campaign cars would be parked next to their beat-up old Dart. Thousands of people would be pushing their way into the warehouse, and he would certainly want to be one of them.

"No," Sylvia said, "I want to get home before tomorrow."

"Come on, let's stay, it'll be fun."

"No."

"Honey, let's."

"No."

"Why not?"

"Look, Leonard, if it means that much to you, you stay and march in the parade and I'll drive home with the kids."

Sylvia imagined Leonard lifting his luggage out of the trunk and handing her the car keys, then waving wildly at the children's faces pressed to the back window as the car pulled away, but he apparently decided that he still had some doubts about McCarthy. For McCarthy was not—Leonard's litmus test—Eugene V. Debs. *While there is a soul in prison, I am not free*: Leonard seemed to believe it. Sylvia knew she was not free, whether or not souls were in prison, but she did like McCarthy. Now Leonard wanted to leave, but the children wanted to see what was in the warehouse and Sylvia wanted to stay and ask the Senator if he remembered her introducing him to the crowd at a fundraising picnic in Pasadena last spring. Walt asked why suddenly McCarthy was good and they were going to give him money when his father had always told him that McCarthy was bad, very bad. As they crossed the street from the parking lot to the warehouse, Sylvia explained to Walt that there were two McCarthys: one was a man with a red nose and jowly chin who, occasionally in old television footage and all the time in his father's fury, asked, "Are you now or have you ever been?" The other McCarthy wrote marvelous little poems to himself and had the most compassionate eyes she'd ever seen.

The warehouse was so dark that when she walked in the door Sylvia felt like a hideaway in the hulk of a ship, and the cement floor was as wet as their Jackson Hole cabin had been and was covered with crushed paper cups, which featured the Senator signing visionary legislation and frolicking with his family. Rusted pipes hung down from the ceiling and pumped steam into the atmosphere, and across all four walls were posters proclaiming MCCARTHY FOR PRESIDENT: A PROMISE FOR PEACE. Promises, Sylvia could practically hear Leonard thinking, lousy liberal promises.

In the far corner of the building a young man was folding up and stacking aluminum chairs, so they walked across the

platform and down a long aisle to ask him why he was putting *away* the chairs. Campaign buttons were pinned to his
pants pockets and his red tie and blue-and-white shirt. Sylvia
wondered what it was she liked so much about belts, although she supposed it was the way they divided men so
neatly in half: top, bottom; teeth, toes; nose, knees; mind,
matter. The campaign worker had intelligent-looking eyes
and wavy black hair.

The McCarthy worker told them he registered voters and
mapped strategy and now was folding up the chairs after
everyone had gone home.

"After?"

"Yeah. The Senator was here and spoke and left late last
night. You didn't think—"

"We came all the way from Los Angeles to see him,"
Leonard said, which Sylvia wanted to explain was in a sense
true and in another sense of course quite false.

The young man could only shake his head and broad
shoulders and say, "I'm sorry, I'm terribly sorry," and offer
them a box of campaign buttons.

Leonard had so wanted to see the Senator and feel a part
of things, but Walt and Ellen were already playing on the
platform, stepping up to the dead microphone and introducing each other and then listening in mock solemnity.

Swerving in and out of his lane, as usual, tailgating the
van in front of him, Leonard drove all the way back to town
to have breakfast at Denny's, where the food was surpris-
ingly good and the cashier, who had purple fingernails and
red hair wrapped high in a bun, asked if they had and when
they said they hadn't she said they must, they absolutely
must, see the Great Salt Lake. "It's not a body of water,"

she said, giving Leonard his change, "it's the fourth wonder of the world."

The children said they wanted to see the fourth wonder of the world because, when they were in Jackson Hole, everyone had told them that the Grand Tetons were the eighth wonder of the world, which meant that the Great Salt Lake was either twice as wondrous or half as wondrous as the Grand Tetons, and in any case they wanted to see it and swim in it very badly. They had an admirable amount of enthusiasm.

Leonard said, "No, definitely not, we have to be getting back."

Sylvia said, "Maybe we will."

Leonard shook his head and clucked his tongue and said *Acch* so many times that Sylvia chided him by asking if he had a sore throat, which had its intended effect of shaming him into driving around downtown until they came to a motel which happened to have both vacancies and an indoor pool. They showered and changed into their swimsuits, and despite Leonard's ludicrous suggestion to stay home and swim in the heated pool, which had a white kickboard floating in the shallow end, they got back in the car and drove a few miles down a dirt road to the Great Salt Lake.

There were fathers with cigars and mothers with bathing caps and children with beach balls, and none of them were drowning. The lake was very clear and very blue and reportedly very warm, and although there were wooden signs stuck into the sand warning swimmers not to open their eyes under water or the thick salt would sting their eyes, even that possibility seemed to Sylvia rather remote. The moment she waded in and flipped over on her back and floated, she realized that the lake was keeping her up. She couldn't sink below the surface even if she wanted to. She puffed out her stomach and kicked her legs and flapped her arms, but she didn't have to be doing anything.

The children floated quite a ways out and Leonard treaded over to her with a tiny black camera, an Olympus Trip 35, strapped around his neck and jammed between the upper and lower set of his false teeth. He took close-ups of her with her hands folded behind her head and her eyes shut in the sun and a sleepy smile across her face. She floated from midday until sunset, always drifting but never too far from shore. Now and then she would be interrupted to squint into Leonard's camera lens or fix Ellen's strap for her or agree with Walt that it was unbelievably cool not to have to think about drowning. For five full hours, she lay on top of this lake of lead in her navy blue swimsuit and her plastic white swimming cap (which Ellen said made her look like Amelia Earhart) until she felt surrounded by shadows. The water around her felt cold and clammy and her feet started to tingle a little, so she frog-kicked toward the beach and stood up when she knew she could touch bottom. She dried off, and when the children returned and Leonard sat up in the sand—he later told her he'd been having the strangest dream about the Dreyfus Affair—they drove back to the motel.

Leonard walked across the parking lot to their room, saying he wanted only to shower, read a little more about the Resistance, and then get some sleep before the long trip home tomorrow morning. Sylvia sat back in a wet lounge chair with the sun bouncing off the glass wall behind her and the smell of pool water seeping into the cracked cement at her feet, and watched the children swim. They seemed to think they could float anywhere now, so they dove into the indoor pool and stayed afloat for a while, but after at most a minute, Walt swallowed some water and swam to the side to catch his breath and a few seconds later Ellen said her stomach muscles were tightening up and her legs ached and she, too, went under. Walt and Ellen were getting tired and floating less and less and sinking more and more. It didn't seem to matter to either of them that the indoor pool was not the Great Salt Lake; when floating was no longer any fun, they dove off the diving board in the deep end and slid down the slide together and walked along the wrinkled plastic floor in the shallow end of the pool. To Sylvia, it made all the difference in the world. She wanted something other than Leonard's photographs of Salt Lake to last. She wanted to like Leonard, the children to float forever, and the lake to wash away a few wounds, but it hadn't. The children were arguing about whose turn it was to use the kickboard; she was sitting alone in a wet lounge chair; and she imagined Leonard thinking, as he got ready for bed, that he could just as easily have been Albert Camus and a contributor to *Combat.*

Heart

of

a

Dybbuk

Although his mother had died almost a year before, Tannenbaum felt that he hadn't yet really grieved. Her cancer had been in remission for quite a while, and when it returned and stayed and stayed, Tannenbaum had been what the university shrink called "curiously without affect." Tannenbaum's mother had noticed this much earlier, and conveyed her feeling in a long, angry letter she wrote to him immediately upon returning home from the hospital. His mother tearfully recanted the letter when she emerged from her drugged state and remembered how effusive and distressed he had been when he first heard the news, but Tannenbaum nevertheless thought his mother had zeroed in on something that was there: his weird detachment. What the hell was the matter with him, anyway—wasn't he human, didn't his heart pump blood like everyone else's?

Now, a year later—1978—Tannenbaum and Nora were traveling by train from Providence to New York to hand-deliver a sepia-tinted photograph to his Aunt Evelyn. Evelyn's husband, who had died many years before, was Tannenbaum's mother's brother. Evelyn had always said how much she "cherished" a particular photograph of Sylvia and Paul as children, and when Tannenbaum's mother had died, this was the only momento Evelyn had requested. So Tannenbaum had had it framed and now was holding in his lap (encased in glass, wrapped in butcher paper) a five-by-eight photograph of Paul at seven, Tannenbaum's mother at four and a half: Paul standing at attention, clean and cooperative, the little gentleman; Tannenbaum's mother, sitting on the edge of a floral-print chair, her socks bunched up, her shoes scuffed, her hair uncombed, looking a mess. Bronze light haloed everything.

Nora finally returned from the snack bar. She told Tannenbaum all about bumping into an old man name Hy Levy, who had a wispy white beard hanging down from his chin and a yarmulke perched on top of his bald head. Having persuaded her to sit down with him in a seat at the back, he had talked and she had listened. He told her about the Lower East Side and the small shul for which he served as administrative secretary and the pitiable whores on Eighth Avenue. He had eloquently conveyed to her his loneliness and poor health, even asked her to feel his heart, which she did: he unbuttoned his coat and puffed out his chest and Nora had put her hand to his shirt pocket, although she felt nothing in particular other than his heartbeat. "Fibrillations," he had said.

She'd heard his story and was moved. She wanted him to accompany them to Aunt Evelyn's for dinner. Was this

just another doomed scheme on her part to goad him—
Tannenbaum—back into life? Probably, probably. "No,"
Tannenbaum said, "he can't come."

And yet (precisely because Tannenbaum was so deficient
in his will to act for or against), when the train stopped at
Penn Station, Levy followed right behind them, shlepping a
huge belted valise. Nora helped him ascend the stairs to the
station which he was having such trouble negotiating, and
he thanked her: took a piece of matzo from his sack and
gave it to her. "Eat," he said, so she ate. She munched while
Levy—Hy Levy, administrative secretary, Union Square
Congregation—introduced himself to Tannenbaum, who
wiped his hand on his trousers after shaking Levy's hand
and turned from obituaries in the newspaper he was reading
to tabloid headlines in papers he wasn't—from death, really,
to more death. "And you," Levy said to him, "you were too
busy to help me up the stairs? 'The face of the generation
is like the face of a dog; brazenness will reign.'"

Tannenbaum ignored him, pretending not to understand. Levy shook his head. Nora laughed. Battalions of the
poor and rich trooped by—such was the extent of Tannenbaum's impression of Penn Station; his involuted consciousness registered next-to-nothing of the famous, physical world.
He did, however, want to know whether Nora was laughing
with him, that is, with Tannenbaum at Levy, in which case
he had nothing to worry about, for he was more than willing
to mock this ridiculous excuse for a rabbi throughout the
journey, or whether Nora was laughing at him, that is, with
Levy at Tannenbaum, in which case he had had quite
enough. Levy complained and clutched his chest, which
prompted Nora to ask him (as a distraction from the pain he
was apparently feeling) questions about the most popular
items in the synagogue gift shop and the layout of his fourth-
floor walk-up, and which prompted Tannenbaum, tactless,

blunt to the point of being cruel, to ask him whether he was in fact dying, to which Levy nodded: Yes. He was all but dead.

He told Nora which subways to take—"The one, two, or three to Times Square, the shuttle to Grand Central, then the four, five, or six uptown; personally, I much prefer the six"—and was really getting going again about the reign of brazenness ("The house of assembly will become a brothel, Galilee will be laid to waste, people will wander from city to city, and none will pity them") when Nora apologized for interrupting him and insisted, against his loud and passionate if ultimately unsuccessful objections, that he not only take the same subway she and Tannenbaum were taking but that he also wind up at the same place to which they were destined: Aunt Evelyn's air-conditioned condominium on the twenty-sixth floor in the East Eighties. Nora pleaded with Levy to come, with Tannenbaum to put down his goddamn newspaper and extend a decent invitation to this wise, wonderful old man; Levy protested entirely too much; and Tannenbaum, aware that Levy might die on the way or while waiting for the elevator in the mirrored lobby and perversely excited by that possibility (excited, too, by the near certainty that Evelyn would despise this half-baked holy man, this glorified mezuzah salesman), wrapped one arm around Levy's frail shoulders and said, "You will come."

Tannenbaum held Levy's dilapidated luggage, Nora held his hand, and Levy talked. He waved his yarmulke, pounded on Nora and Tannenbaum, placed undue stress upon his heart. He spoke a staccato English punctuated with flurries of Yiddish whenever things got interesting, so that as the story grew progressively more complicated—a "balshem" or wonder-worker was involved, as were talismans, a yellow cat, a dybbuk, the village of Volhynia, amulets, a white satin coat, a container of "pitch," demons, daughters; Tannenbaum could hardly keep any of it straight—Nora, deaf in the sense that she had no ear for idiom, could no more comprehend what Levy was saying than fly. Out of necessity rather than choice, she turned to Tannenbaum for help, for a little support if that wasn't too much to ask, but he only laughed, clapped Levy on the back, and told Nora she had to pick up what she could on her own and forget about story line.

Levy paused in the telling of this potentially interminable tale to walk down the steps to the subway with them, or actually, was helped down the steps by Nora—by Nora, again, because this time Tannenbaum was busy with his latest horoscope. "Meshuggener," Levy said, limping, with one hand on the steel rail and one hand grasping Nora's outstretched and benevolent arm. "These three things only come unawares: the Messiah, a found article, a scorpion." Which very nearly revolutionized Tannenbaum's thinking because he had not only just read but believed that, as a Scorpio, he should strive to place renewed emphasis on close personal relationships and attempt to avoid wearing either purple or dark red.

Nora and the old man struggled their way past beggars and businessmen to the bottom of the stairs. In front of the turnstiles, Levy went so far as to pour the contents of his pants pockets onto the filthy concrete to show that he'd misplaced his change purse. Somewhere on his journey back from a sister synagogue in Boston, the leather pouch had supposedly been stolen and now he didn't know where it was. He turned around and asked Tannenbaum, "Do I look like the kind of person that would cheat you? I don't have a penny. You, with so much money, it wouldn't kill you to do a good deed for a fellow human being whose heart is out of kilter permanently until he dies, which, so far as I know, may be tomorrow." Followed inevitably by some more reign-of-brazenness stuff: " 'Boys will shame old men and old men will show deference to boys. The son reviles the father, the daughter rises up against—"

Nora said, "Hy, please. Please don't talk that way," and Tannenbaum, more than a bit meshugge ever since his mother's death, in that he had taken to rubbing rare and exquisite headstones at night and chasing fire engines to scenes of ruin by day, secretly hoped for or at least eagerly awaited Levy's demise and yet he was compassionate enough to lend Levy a couple of pieces of silver, which he accepted with gratitude and the promise of repayment plus interest. An uptown subway pulled into the station as they passed through the turnstiles, and Tannenbaum, holding Levy's bag, told him to run so they could catch the train, but Nora tugged on Levy's arm and said to him, "Don't you dare exert yourself, Hy. Don't listen to him. With your heart giving you so much trouble, you shouldn't overdo it. We're in no hurry." Levy implied agreement, shuffling his feet in place, while Tannenbaum sprinted to the subway and pounded on the steel door of the train with his fist, but the door was sealed shut.

Levy nudged someone over and, on the edge of a bench, sat and rested and entertained Tannenbaum and Nora (and, beyond them, everyone else waiting for a train) with the conclusion of the tale he had introduced earlier. The balshem, or wonder-worker, is summoned to drive a dybbuk out of a villager's daughter. She can't sleep at night and keeps shrieking that there's a demon in her featherbed. The balshem takes a yellow cat, smears it with pitch, cuts open the featherbed, inserts the cat, carries the woman's bed into the woods. Incantations, promises, whispers, chants from Kabbalah, a lot of spitting. The balshem beats the featherbed; the cat, blackened with pitch, leaps out of the bed, "yowling." The young woman sees that the dybbuk has fled, grows calm, and can now sleep at night. She recovers her health. "Hear, O Israel!"

Tannenbaum's only response was to make an elaborate show of fishing a tabloid out of the nearest garbage bin and folding it open to the race results. Nora snatched the paper out of his hands and asked, "Why can't you be nice to Hy? He's dying, for God's sake. You've got a real, live example of imminent death here, but you can't deal with that, can you? Only artifacts and magazines and obituaries? Why must it always be me who comes to you and begs you to respond? Do you care? Why can't we simply take a trip for once and get along and be nice to each other and nice to other people?"

Nora's plaintive tone, her series of self-righteous questions, her self-conscious delivery of rehearsed material, all this moved Tannenbaum profoundly and he cried, or if he didn't cry, he laughed. Somewhere halfway between the two probably; he honestly couldn't tell which. He and Nora proceeded to delineate each other's character flaws, expressing veiled disgust and later outright repugnance and finally physical violence toward each other's bodies (Nora kept shaking him by the shoulders; he kept shrugging her off) and questioning the relationship itself—whether it was indeed love—until the framed photograph flew right out of Tannenbaum's hands, skidding across the platform into the canyon of the train tracks. Everyone glanced at Tannenbaum and Nora, then turned away. A yellow light flashed from the darkness of the tunnel. The subway rattled down the tracks in the distance—the number 2 train: recommended by Levy.

Levy stood up off the bench with a start and stumbled toward Tannenbaum and Nora, both of whom must have appeared to Levy to be on the verge of scrambling after the lost artifact. Six weeks later, when Tannenbaum called the number Levy wrote down for them, he found out that fibrillations had become attack; Levy was dead. A month after that, Tannenbaum and Nora broke up, temporarily but rancorously. Now, though, Levy kneeled next to them and spoke what to Tannenbaum's ears sounded like the only wisdom he'd ever heard: "Oh, taste and see that the Lord is good." Then, of course, Levy had to ruin it by elaborating: "Not He who is good but that which is good. For how is it possible to say of God that He is good? Would that not mean that . . ." Nora turned, smiling, toward Tannenbaum—apparently to receive thanks for her part in nudging him out of his numb little hell. Tannenbaum gathered she had somehow been able to see it in his face the second he felt it in his heart—which was that for the first time since he'd first met Nora three years ago in a Portuguese bakery in the Fox Point section of Providence, when he told her he was "inconsolably attracted" to her, Tannenbaum's capillaries were open for business. The world rushed in on him. His eyes were aimed at the ground; he was bowing with maniacal rapidity; and he was speaking loud, elliptical Hebrew in perfect concert with Levy.

Comp Lit 101: Walt Grows Up

The origin of enslavement is
the invention of writing.

FOUCAULT

Good to get your long and candid letter, Walt. I must say
I'm somewhat perplexed by your reaction to your creative
writing class—I think you have the accent on the wrong
syllable, figuratively speaking. You're in this class to learn
from the teacher, and perhaps from your fellow students. I
think if you keep this in mind you'll loosen up a bit and get
a great deal out of the course. All of your classmates are in
the same boat; they're all just as apprehensive about reveal-
ing themselves as you are, even though some may be able
to camouflage it better than others. I think it's great you
were accepted in the class, and you should think so, too.
Relax, and learn from this "famous" writer (though I don't
know his books and had never heard of him before). A cer-

tain amount of fear and anxiety at the approach of a new experience is natural and healthy. I don't know any placid types who are creative people; intensity is what drives them to the outrageous thoughts and ideas ordinary people never think of. But anxiety also has to be self-controlled if it's not to become the dominant force.

I find Kosinski a good writer, very good. Nobody I've read recently writes a better, simpler declarative sentence—no extraneous language, not one extra word or sentiment. With your stuff I'm sometimes so busy untangling the syntax I don't know what you want to say.

Not to be involved with mankind is not to have lived; join up.

The Roth book you gave me for my birthday (thank you) grew on me. At first I did a foolish thing: I placed my own prejudices ahead of the novel. I wanted Roth to leave, for good, his absorption with his father and mother and their self-deprecation. I wanted him also to leave the novel told in the first person. Why doesn't he write novels like every-one else? Writing them in the first person is the lazy way, the easier way. I soon realized how utterly naive and unso-phisticated such an attitude was and settled down to enjoy the book, even that very contrived exchange of letters be-tween David and Debbie, and David and Arthur.

Why not take the reader into your confidence rather then play a game of wits with him?

. . .

I'm hoping that you won't wait as long as I did to learn how to make dinner, clean house, do a sensible marketing, make household purchases, etc., etc. Just because one is a "poet" doesn't mean one has to be a shlemiel. I feel very strongly about this and look forward to talking about it in depth sometime.

The Front? I didn't like it. The blacklistings were serious. I want serious subjects treated seriously.

I went with your great-uncle Hyman to hear Elie Wiesel give a talk at UCLA this week. A very moving experience, comparable only to the talk I heard by Chaim Potok several years ago. Wiesel had been in Auschwitz as a teenager and so, of course, he spoke about the Holocaust and the violence and the baffling faith of the Jewish people in humanity. He opened with a tale of two Russian peasants who were sitting around drinking and talking. Jacob says to his friend Yosal, "Are you my friend?" "Of course," Yosal assures him. They talk some more and again Jacob asks Yosal if he's his friend and again Yosal assures him. Then Jacob asks him once more, "Are you really my friend?" And Yosal says, "Of course I am, why do you keep asking?" "Well," replies Jacob, "if you are my friend, how come you don't know that I am hurting?" Then Wiesel closed his talk by quoting from documents that he saw recently, diaries and journals written by concentration-camp victims who were forced to conduct their fellow Jews into the gas ovens and then later were themselves incinerated. They left letters and notes and descriptions in bottles and boxes in crevices in the crematoria—some discovered only now. If ever there were people who had the right to tell all the world to go to hell, these were such people. But instead they wanted humanity to know what had happened there, and by sharing their experiences and describing them they demonstrated their faith in the survival of the Jews and their faith that people would remember and not ever let such horrors happen again. It was a very respectful, silent, and appreciative audience, and there wasn't a dry eye in the house; Hyman went through two handkerchiefs himself.

Don't stop the world because you want to get off.

A play—even a one-act set in seventeenth-century England—needs some "wasted" moments to make it work. Your protagonist, Lilburne, is alone way too much. Plus, he's a pompous martyr; he couldn't have been that self-righteous in real life. I want to see him in private, enjoying himself with his family, being witty. So far he's so serious as to be inhuman. Work it out in *emotional* terms, not intellectual ones.

It's been a long time since I've seen you. You've done a lot of greening and growing in the fourteen months since you were last here. I think I've done some, too. My old habits have been carted off to the dump. You'll see, I think, when you visit in March, although I thought I detected at the end of our last conversation a very conscious pulling-away on your part—a rejection of me—when I offered to put you up in this very spacious apartment.

. . .

John William Corrington writes in the darkly humorous tradition of a Barth, Donleavy, or Heller. He is concerned with the troubled spirit of this country and writes about it with gusto.

Peace in the world or the world in pieces.

I found that toward the end of summer I needed some distance between you and me because I was becoming so conscious of your writing, presumably about me. When you told me that, after dinner with me and Hyman, you went downstairs and recorded our sodden trip down memory lane, I was disturbed by it, and after that I felt you were making mental or actual notes anytime anything of an "interesting" or curious nature was discussed between me and Hy. I don't mind that you use any of your observations about me in your writing, but I do mind being made so conscious of the fact that you're doing it. If other people get this feeling, you may find that they, too, require distance from you, and this doesn't make for close, open, honest relationships. I've known quite a few writers and have never had the feeling with them that they were interested in me or observing me just for what grist I could provide for their mill. This is an attitude and approach that I think you will, in time, learn to cultivate.

Some think O'Hara's stories consisted of an introduction, a little character development, and the rest was dialogue of a most ordinary nature. O'Hara was more than that, much more. He said the lonely mind of the artist is the only creative organ in the world. His advice: inherit money, have a job that will keep you busy, be born without a taste for liquor, join a church, don't live too long. Oh, he had his wild and uncontrollable moments. He thought of his work as a personal reassessment against the history of his time. He was an important writer of the '20s, '30s, and the '40s and clear until the time he died.

I know from your letters and even the things you say to me during our too-brief telephone conversations that a real maturing, even a toughness, has taken place and I know it'll be very much in evidence in what you write.

This blacklisted writer (played by Luther Adler, I think, maybe not), after coming out of jail for contempt of a Congressional committee, gets some work in the gray market and then has a chance to do a script on his own. He can't believe his luck has changed. Then, just as he's about to sign the contract, his friend comes to his place and says, "Well, it seems that somebody has been doing some poking around and you know how it is, this ain't the end of the world, times will change, you'll see, one of these days we'll look back on all this and laugh, but in the meantime you're off the picture and we have to put some shnook, a nebbish who can't carry your typewriter ribbon, on the picture." Adler looks at him, looks through him, and on Adler's face is written all of man's grief from the beginning of time. His friend sees him to the door, arm languidly on his shoulder—feeble gesture of phony friendship, but it's there. And he asks Adler, "What will you do now? What will you do?" Adler says three words, and no more eloquent words have ever been spoken on screen, stage, TV, or anywhere: "Survive. I'll survive." He closes the door and walks off into the night. The scene haunts me still and I bet I saw it on Playhouse 90 twenty-five years ago, maybe longer. That's real writing.

Illumine the human condition—that's all. Set it down one little word after another. No tricks or gimmicks.

Did you know I must have tried half a dozen times to get down on paper those stories Hyman told you and me about being a panhandler in New York during the Depression? I never could get away from the plain reportage of it, even though I strove to put in "local color" and the "bums" as Hy depicted them. But, on my now-and-then tries, I couldn't get past the obligatory opening scenes—descriptions of the Lower East Side, etc. Rarely got much further. "Fiction is not fact," wrote Thomas Wolfe (the real Thomas Wolfe). "Fiction is fact, selected and charged with a purpose." Which is exactly what you did—blending Hy's memories with your imagination to put together an absorbing story. I can't begin to tell you how much it moved me, especially the very end when Tannenbaum says Kaddish. Beyond my poor powers of description. (One minor criticism: why do you need such a cutesy title? How many people nowadays even know what a dybbuk is? Why not just something simple like "A Boy Grows Up"?)

Contemporary

Film

Criticism

Nina and I go to another movie about love overcoming numerous obstacles. She shushes the movie crowd, raucous on vacation. I admire only the dialogue I can't quite catch. Toward the end, the hero's friend's suicide allows everyone in the audience to die but live. Afterward, thinking the car is stolen, I yelp in the empty, misty parking lot. (In the trunk are my birthday presents for her.) She finally sees where we're parked. Driving with bad brakes on the slick street, I slide through a stop sign, turning 180 degrees, hopping the curb. Angry at my careless driving, she jumps out of the car and I give her ten seconds to get back in. She refuses. Gallantly, as in Italian neorealism, I leave in order to return, but when I return, the car hydroplanes again toward the sidewalk, nearly killing our appetite for more movies.

Ode

to

the

Donner

Party

Now that they had no one else to talk to, my mother and
father took long hikes in the woods together and went to
chamber-music concerts and treated each other to dinner
when either of them could afford it. They still fought, of
course—one night she kicked him out of the house and
didn't let him back in until the weekend was over—and she
was still getting used to buying two little bags of groceries
rather than four full ones, but that would change. He'd fall
asleep early, snoring in the living room with a magazine
folded across his chest, and awake at sunrise to run around
the block a few times before he went to work. She'd stay up
late, watching PBS and writing letters—to me, to my sister,
to historians at UCLA, Berkeley, and Stanford who corrected errors in the articles she wrote for the state historical

society's monthly magazine. But my parents would see each other at dinner and often had long and heated conversations about philosophy or politics or money, which usually ended in both of them leaving the house and stomping around the front lawn until it got dark.

She saw no point in going to all the bother of making a lavish dinner for just the two of them, so she'd bake a few blintzes or scramble some eggs or warm up leftovers and he would say, "This is dinner?" He'd throw down his napkin and, according to my mother, drive to the most expensive restaurant in town, where, while correcting page proofs for the suburban weekly he edited, he would wolf down the specialties of the house and charge it to his business account. Or, if he stayed and they didn't argue, they'd stare at their plates and nibble their food. Hardly a word would pass between them: only the sounds of chewing and swallowing, the dog padding through the house, coughs filling the silence, the cold clank of utensils doing their routine work. And after dinner they'd fight like little children about who would clean the table and who would scrape the dishes. Who would rinse? Who would stack? Who would take out the garbage? Who would wipe the table? Who indeed? And every night this absurdity was enacted.

Weekends they would rake, water, and mow the lawn and trim the hedges, but he would always leave the water running and flood the lawn, or she'd cut the grass so unevenly that it looked like an aerial shot of the Midwestern states. My mother would march onto the front lawn and say, "See, Leonard, this is how you rake. It's very simple. You rake the leaves off the lawn into a pile in the gutter, then you put them in a barrel. Any idiot can do it." Or he'd drag the hose from the backyard and attach it to a spigot underneath the front porch, and squatting down and placing his thumb over the nozzle, spray the water low and full through the top of the grass so the lawn looked cool and fresh. "See, honey," he would say, "is this so hard? Why is this so difficult for you?" They never had any answers, so they'd swear at each other or shake their heads or shake each other. Sometimes, my father said, they'd fall to their knees together and pound the earth, tearing out grass.

All day Saturday, she would clean the house and he would track mud across a carpet she had just vacuumed. She'd scatter newspapers—often copies of *his* newspaper—across the waxed linoleum and he'd be very careful to walk in the spaces in between the papers. Never would he think to come in the back door or notice that the kitchen floor had been mopped and was wet. Sometimes she would get so mad she'd throw the mop at him. Sometimes she simply screamed.

Saturday nights they would disagree about what movie to see and then disagree about the movie. He would get lost driving there, then park on the wrong side of the street. He would forget to bring his glasses so they'd have to sit near the front, and then, after going to the bathroom, he would lose his ticket stub and forget to zip up his zipper. He would walk up and back in the aisle because he wouldn't be able to find the row and she would have to whisper, "Over here, Leonard." He'd squirm in his seat, ask her questions about plot, hold his head when he got tired, get hard during sex scenes, play with his false teeth. "Leonard," she would say, "do you have to do that—would your head really fall off if you didn't hold it?" If he liked the movie, she would find it manipulative and sentimental; if he disliked it, she'd think it was original and provocative.

Or, if they didn't go to a movie, they would go to a party, where my father would back into a corner whomever he could and talk about the Rosenbergs or Alger Hiss or Sacco and Vanzetti or Alfred Dreyfus or the Hollywood Ten. And, if he got drunk enough, he would tell stories in Yiddish, but no one would listen because this was my mother's crowd. These weren't recent East European immigrants; these were American Jews who had made it a long time ago—lawyers and professors and psychiatrists who didn't want to hear about the old country. My mother would laugh and gossip, and my father would wander away from the crowd and collapse on a bed in the guest room with a Picasso picture book at his side. She would wake him when the party was over, and driving home, she would accuse him of being socially illiterate, which was an exaggeration but had some basis in fact: he had a way of standing very close to you and talking very loud and poking his finger into your chest to make sure you got the point.

Sunday, though, provided a respite from all this ugliness. She would make a big breakfast for him and he would let her have the sections of the newspaper she most highly prized. Then they would change into their tennis whites. She would wear a big, floppy hat to protect her skin from the sun, and he would wear a tight cap to cover his head and prevent the sun from blinding him when he hit overhead smashes. Hand in hand they would walk to the park, where they had reserved a court, and they would rally back and forth to get warmed up. She could neither bend low nor move more than a few flat-footed steps in any direction, but put a ball waist high and in front of her and she could sock it, so he'd try to hit the ball directly at her, and if he hit it a few inches too high or half a step out of her way, she'd wave at it with her racquet and glower at him. Usually they would play mixed doubles against another couple and my father would want to win so badly he would rush onto her side of the court to take shots away from her. Whenever this happened, she would take exceedingly long water breaks.

My father would send me every issue of his weekly newspaper, which I was supposed to read thoroughly, mark up
with my comments, and mail back to him. His paper consisted almost exclusively of advertising, and what few stories
he wrote were usually features about local merchants who
were not yet advertising. He wrote long windy sentences
that recalled, he thought, early Mencken. One of his sentences which I have always remembered went:

> With the city fathers giving their official blessings—
> and some 250 mothers and fathers seated in the bleachers,
> giving their partial blessings and vociferous cheers—the
> city soccer players launched their season on Saturday
> with a bang or, more accurately, a boot.

He'd take photographs for the paper with his Polaroid camera, but he never learned how to roll on the gloss or when
to peel off the backing, and the pictures always turned out
fuzzy and faded, like very late Mencken.

My mother didn't send me the articles (which were always odes to the Watts Towers or John Steinbeck or the
Donner Party) that she wrote for the historical society magazine. Instead, she'd type up passages from novels she was
reading and mail them to me. The passages would always be
extremely pejorative summaries of a male character who re-
minded my mother of my father; this paragraph from Wal-
lace Stegner's *The Spectator Bird* is a perfect example:

> Joe Allston has always been full of himself, uncer-
> tain, dismayed, dissatisfied with his life, his country, his
> civilization, his profession, and himself. He has always
> hunted himself in places where he has never been, he
> has always been trying to thread some needle with a
> string that was raveled at both ends. He has always been

hungry for some continuity and assurance and sense of belonging, but has never had ancestors or descendants or place in the world. Little orphan Joe, what a sad case.

I was a freshman at Brown—an almost unfathomably serious English major—and my sister was a law student at Yale. We would write letters to each other in which we expressed our pity for people such as our parents who thrived on chewing up the furniture; our determination to avoid similarly disastrous entanglements in our own lives; and our certainty that our correspondence would someday be valuable because we were both destined to become famous in the fields of literature and politics. What did we know? We were nineteen and twenty-three, respectively, and knew nothing yet of love.

Babies

Curt is small but, as Nina often said in assault against my big body, "wiry." Everybody wears letter jackets; Curt is wearing his bona fide high school jacket, though, from autumn Arkansas afternoons as a wiry wide receiver. I'm wearing bowling shoes, very Melrose Avenue. Nina and I used to live two blocks north of Melrose, but east of La Brea, in pseudo-Spanish stucco. Once, when we actually went bowling, she criticized me for lining up my feet with the toe marks, cradling the ball, taking it so seriously. That was when we lived in pseudo-Spanish stucco and Nina taped a photograph of me, age eight with red Halloween horns, to her notebook. "Not to be too self-conscious about this or anything," Curt is saying, "but I like you and am glad I like you." "I know so much about you," I have to say (Nina still tells me almost everything); "I know things about you you don't even know." In Curt's journal, for instance, he was partial to defining love as a potentially subversive activity. The baby behind us keeps sticking his stubby digits into my moussed-up hair until I ask his mother to have him stop. A girl at the table, a former girlfriend's former boyfriend's new girlfriend, cries, cries. We get Curt's new girlfriend's brother drunk enough to tell us about Brooke Shields at Princeton: "She'd walk by in her sweatshirt and we'd all gurgle like babies." Curt and I attempt to but can't talk about what we want to talk about: first I, then he, was engaged to Nina. I court a girl named Paige from Marina Del Rey and miss Nina's distance, the impossibility she created you couldn't bridge. Just now, intending to type "bridge," I first typed "bride." A few summers ago, in an unlikely attempt to win her anorexic heart back, I did wind sprints, then started reading *Bride's* magazine at the dentist's office. In L.A. people get their teeth bonded; Heather Locklear, for instance, met her husband, Tommy Lee, the drummer for Mötley Crüe, at the dentist's. Now they both have extremely white teeth. The boyfriend of the girl who is crying says to Curt, "You're a man's man." Curt says, "Well, I also try to be a gentleman as well." What is the common denominator of melancholy, desire, regret, and jealousy? The glamour of absence. (Nina organized this little reunion of her former fiancés, but of course she never showed.) I wasn't a wiry wide receiver in Arkansas. I played second-string guard on my horrible high school basketball team. I start dropping my g's. An Hermosa Beach blonde, unsteady in cowboy boots, dips her hand into my jacket pocket. She's vial seeking, but Curt thinks she just wanted to dance and we follow her into the parking lot, where he mouths the question and she writes "A+" in the air of her van, grading his profile. Curt once wrote Nina, "You're a wonderful romantic scenarist, but you were no better than I was at living it out." He wrote maybe a dozen letters like that, explaining what he meant. This is nothing compared to my correspondence. Nina did dance exercises in her chamois teddy in our pseudo-Spanish stucco, eating Mint Milano cookies, using my back as her barre. Curt's new girlfriend asks, "What does 'inculcate' mean?" Paige and I walk on the sand at midnight, when the ocean is of no use anymore to anybody. This is what it was like out on Catalina over Christmas.

Interference

Sylvia had packed a suitcase full of presents for her family—a transistor radio for Walt, a marionette for Ellen, a book about the Rosenbergs for Leonard—and who else would have thought to give rather than expect gifts after serious surgery? She insisted on returning with a smile: upbeat, even cheerful. She was also bringing home every flower that had been absorbing sunlight in her room because Ellen loved flowers, so the nurse carried them out to Sylvia on the sidewalk.

Leonard placed the suitcases and flowers in the backseat and bent down to carry her into the front seat until she explained she wasn't crippled, she could walk. The nurse released the footrest and Sylvia's legs swung swiftly down, but she was surprised how much she hurt as she stepped gingerly toward the car and eased herself, holding the door, into the front seat. The nurse said, "We don't want to see you back here ever again," and not until the end of the week did it occur to Sylvia that she may have meant this in a nice way.

She saw the black butts of her own cigarettes in the ashtray. The glove compartment was open and empty like a big black mouth, the leather seats spilled foam rubber, the speedometer flashed red until he slowed down. She tried to remember what the car had looked like new. The windshield wipers screeched across the window, spreading dirt. She sat straight in her seat and looked at Leonard, whose sunglasses were perched like green goggles on top of his bald head. Little gray hairs stuck out of his ears, and long gray hairs poked out from the twin tufts of his eyebrows. He was wearing his sweatshirt and loosely laced sneakers, so he must already have run to the park and back.

Leonard drove past the nicer places where most of their friends lived—big, square two-story houses white as wedding cakes, with orange trees in front and pools in back. The car coasted down the embankment into the carport, a red tile floor surrounded by wooden posts, which supported the roof, and white cabinets that contained nothing. Leonard honked the horn.

"Don't honk."

He honked again.

"Please, don't honk. You'll disturb the neighbors."

He pounded his palm on the rubber nose of the horn and said, "Relax, honey, this is a celebration."

Pogo bounded out the back door with his uncut claws stretched to scratch as he pranced at the top of the steps, rising up on his hind legs, pawing at the pavement, waiting for Sylvia to make a move. Then came the children in their wool pajamas and warm bathrobes.

"Mom's home," Ellen said.

"Mom, Mom," Walt said, jumping up and down and hitting his hands over his head.

Ellen whispered something to Walt as they waited for her to open the car door and wriggle out of the front seat, and Walt nodded and then both of them rushed toward her with their arms open. "We missed you, Mother," Ellen said very seriously, apparently thinking this was the proper thing to say and the proper way to say it.

Walt tugged at Sylvia's sleeve and asked, "How are you? How are you?"

"She's doing fine," Leonard said.

"You look good," Ellen said.

"How are you?" Walt asked.

"She's never looked better," Leonard said.

Ellen stood on her right side and planted a kiss on her neck and Walt leapt into her arms, but she couldn't hold him for long. Pogo barked at the children and snapped at Sylvia's legs, so Leonard led him into the house and Walt followed, dragging two suitcases. Sylvia clutched wooden posts to steady herself as she stumbled up the porch steps. Ellen shouted: "Flowers."

Sylvia thought the house would be dirty, and when, instead, she saw it was clean she knew she hadn't been missed. Ellen had probably cooked and cleaned and Walt had probably walked Pogo and dumped the garbage and Leonard had probably read the paper. Warm loads of laundry were neatly folded on top of the washing machine and helpful little lists were taped to the side of the refrigerator. The entire house had been dusted, swept, vacuumed, mopped, waxed. The curtains were clean and the windows were washed. Sylvia limped into the living room, collapsing on her favorite couch.

She asked Walt to bring her the heavy suitcase, and since he couldn't seem to distinguish between the two suitcases, he set both of them at her feet. Pogo jumped back and forth from the floor onto the couch, chewing her slippers and sniffing for food, while Ellen went around watering all the flowers her mother had brought home. Sylvia sat up and opened a suitcase, which contained nothing but clothes, then opened the other one, reached down, and gave Walt a cardboard box wrapped in white paper.

"Honey, this isn't right. We should be giving *you* gifts," Leonard said cheerfully.

Walt ripped the paper and tore open the bottom of the box. He held up a transistor radio, which he said would give him the Dodgers game and Pete Seeger, and played with the dials, turning up the volume all the way, passing through every channel, but there was no sound, not even static.

"Tomorrow," Leonard said, "we'll buy batteries."

Shaking his head, he unwrapped his present: *The Judgment of Julius and Ethel Rosenberg*, the first edition hardcover. There was no subject he knew better or cared more passionately about, no political figure he admired more than Ethel Rosenberg, no villain he hated more than David Greenglass. This particular book Sylvia knew he'd already read three or four times, but he'd never actually owned a copy, and he laid it across his lap and immediately started poring over the appendices and the black-and-white pictures of the jailhouse. He tried to explain to the children how he knew the Rosenbergs were innocent, but Walt was looking for batteries and Ellen was fixing the flowers, waiting for her reward.

Sylvia handed her a marionette, which had red lips and tiny white teeth and orange hair. The doll wore beads around her neck and a loose gown that was supposed to be silk. Ellen read aloud the instructions, which indicated that within hours the serious student should be able to make the marionette blow smoke from a pipe, develop an enormous nose, and become very tall and thin or short and fat, but Ellen couldn't even get the doll to wave hello. She turned the wooden crossbars and pulled on the thin waxed threads, but its shoulders were attached to the lower section of the crossbars while the legs were attached to the upper section, which caused the marionette to move in spasms, the legs going left while the arms swung right, the stomach protruding when the shoulders swung back. She pulled this string, then that one, and watched the puppet's feet flop forward and mouth pop open in silence.

"Stop it," Sylvia said. "Don't play with it until you know how to work it. Stop it, honey."

Ellen lifted the crossbars above her head and swung the doll through the air, its gaudy gown slit open in back and dragging.

Walt had found a couple of dead batteries somewhere and sat down on the living-room rug, installing dry cells in his radio and holding it to his ear, expecting at least some line noise, some faint interference. Leonard put down the book and spoke. "Of what were the Rosenbergs guilty?" he asked.

Walt answered, "Nothing."

"Of being Jews?"

Walt said, "Yes."

Ellen moved the marionette's mouth: "Yes."

"Yes," Leonard said, "and by a Jewish judge." He showed the children pictures of the Jewish judge, Sing Sing, an enormous chair.

"Please, Leonard," Sylvia said, "not now."

She looked out the window, saw that the fog had lifted and the rain had let up, and she wanted to lie down on the lounge in the patio, to feel the sun on her white face. Leonard held her around the waist as she stood up, but she said, "I don't need any help," wriggling out of his grasp and sidestepping the box of batteries and sleeping puppet.

Pogo pushed open the door to the patio and the family followed. Everything was clear and clean, and for the first time she felt she really saw the colors of the patio—the strong green of the hedges. She shut her eyes, and breathing in blue air, pretended it was last year and she was healthy and hiking the High Sierras. Although the sun was high overhead, she was cold, so she called to Ellen to bring her a heavy sweater.

Sylvia leaned over, with only slight discomfort, and looked at the little garden growing along the sides of the sunporch. Ellen had been tending the tomato plants for her while she was away, though she had never told her to, and, seeing that the tomatoes were doing better, really, than she had ever been able to do with them, she suddenly felt happy to be home and flushed with appreciation for her family, especially Ellen. This was where she belonged: outdoors and in the daylight, not being wheeled up and back the loud corridors of a hopeless hospital. She suddenly believed, too, that after a few months of treatments she would be well again. Ellen handed her the sweater, then went right back into the house to continue making lunch.

Sylvia held on to the armrest as she lowered herself into the lounge, rattling the aluminum bars. The mattress was a little damp, and she didn't like the feel of the crinkly plastic or the big white buttons that dotted the mattress and rubbed against her legs as she settled back, but still it felt good to sit in the sun and watch the hummingbirds. Leonard handed her his sunglasses so she wouldn't have to squint when she looked up. Through his goggles she saw the sky as a shallow green sea and the sun as a blue floodlight.

Pogo leapt onto the lounge and bit buttons until Sylvia said, "Go away."

Leonard grabbed his collar, pulling him down, saying, "Git, Pogo, now git out of here."

"So," Sylvia said, sighing, "tell me, Walt, what have you been doing while I've been gone?"

"Nothing."

"Nothing? You must have been doing something."

"Not much."

"Not much of what?"

"Nothing."

"Not much of what?"

"Playing."

"Playing what?"

"Everything."

"What's everything?"

"Everything everyone else plays."

"Have you been good while I've been gone?"

"Yes."

"You have?"

He nodded, but she knew he didn't like it when she made him explain himself. "What did they do to you while you were gone?" he asked her.

"Walt," Leonard said, squeezing his hand, "what kind of question is that to ask your mother?"

Leonard was supposed to have told the children and he hadn't. Sometimes he said it was a nodule on her neck, other times it was a benign tumor on her tummy, but he hadn't told them. He said he didn't have the heart. Ellen she would tell, but who would tell Walt if his father couldn't? She looked into his eyes and lifted up his hidden chin but couldn't bring herself to tell him, either. What was the matter with Leonard? Why hadn't he told him?

Walt suddenly jumped up and ran to the little lemon tree standing in a square plot of dirt at the edge of the patio, pulled down all the lemons he could reach, and cradled them in his arms.

"Would you like me to make some lemonade?" he asked first Sylvia and then Leonard.

Sylvia said, "No thank you."

Leonard said, "Come sit down, Walt."

Walt tossed a lemon to his mother from a few feet away. He knew she always liked to test them.

"Catch," Walt said, and she did catch the lemon, but it was rotten and it squished into a pulp in her hands.

Leonard turned on the garden hose at a trickle to rinse her hands, but he turned the knob left rather than right when he turned off the faucet and the water hit hard on her hands, first fizzling in the nozzle and then flushing out with loud force in a steady stream until he finally turned it off.

She wiped off her hands on the mattress and said she'd like to be left alone, so Walt jumped on his bike to go buy batteries and Leonard went inside to read about the Rosenbergs. Sylvia adjusted the chair so she could lie flat on her back and relax. The doctor had told her not to expose herself to the sun unless she wore a huge hat, but she didn't see how a few minutes in the fresh air could cause any harm. Besides, it felt good to close her eyes and rest and dream. She was on the verge of sleep when Ellen announced out the kitchen window that lunch was ready.

War

Wounds

North Vietnamese or Vietcong forces shot down an Air Vietnam commercial airliner over the Central Highlands, killing all twenty-six people aboard. Pasadena Superior Judge Walter Evans sentenced Billy Joe Booker to death in the gas chamber for abducting a Monrovia woman and her fourteen-month-old daughter from a shopping-center parking lot and then beating them to death with a seventeen-pound rock. According to the Bureau of Land Management, the recent Barstow-to-Las-Vegas motorcycle race destroyed vegetation and substantially reduced small-animal population in the high desert region of southern California. The 16,000-ton tanker *July Star* broke in two and sank off the coast of Algiers; there was no sign of the crew of thirty-five. Although air strikes and mining were prohibited under the Paris agreement ending U.S. involvement in Vietnam, General William Westmoreland, former U.S. military commander in Vietnam, said that President Ford should be given authority to launch B-52 air strikes in Indochina and mine the Haiphong harbor because, according to Westmoreland, the only language Hanoi understood was the language of force.

And that was the good news, because the bad news was that the Selective Service System had just held its national lottery, establishing the random-sequence lottery numbers of all men who had reached or would reach age nineteen during the calendar year 1975: Gookus and me, among others. Everyone who had a lottery number above the administrative processing number would remain 1-H, the holding classification, and would not be subject to further Selective Service processing, while everyone who had received a lottery number equal to or below the administrative processing number would be reclassified into a category available for induction. In the event the military draft was resumed, these men would be in the first group for possible call-up next year; each year after that, they'd fall into a lower priority until they were no longer liable for the draft, normally at age twenty-six. Anyone born in 1956 who did not yet know his lottery number could call the radio station. The car careened.

Jesus Christ, Gookus said. Watch where you're going, man.

Fucking news, I said.

What news?

Weren't you listening? The lottery, Gookus. I bet I got number one.

Just don't register.

I already did.

Idiot.

I thought you had to. I thought they threw you in jail if you didn't.

Think about it: the war's been over for years; why would they even bother to catch up with you?

Didn't you register?

Hell, no.

I turned off the street onto a shoulder and drove across an empty lot, parking next to a phone booth. I'm going to call, I said and got out. Gookus followed close behind and we jammed into the booth. February fourth, he said as I dropped a dime into the coin slot and dialed the radio station. The lower pane of glass in the door was punched out. The phone book, hanging from a short metal chain, was shredded. Memoranda on the metal wall suggested that Michelle was not only good but insatiable, and Gookus tried to memorize her number by saying it softly over and over to himself.

A lady at the radio station said, Hey, listen. This is, like, a radio station. Call the Army.

On the news a few minutes ago the announcer said people could call the station and find out what lottery number they got.

I have the paper in front of me. My boyfriend got 339. Let me find the chart. Okay, man, what's your birthday?

I've got two for you. A friend's with me.

Really, you don't have to ask for me, Gookus said. I don't care.

July twenty-third, I said.

Two-seventy-eight, she said, and I told Gookus, who karate-chopped the wall in joy.

I told her my birthday.

Oh, she said.

Oh?

What a shame.

It's that bad?

I looked at your birthday and I looked at the number. Looked at your birthday, looked at the number. You're number nineteen, man. I'm sorry.

I hung up.

What's the matter? Gookus said. Did you get a low number?

Nineteen.

Are you serious?

Yes.

Gookus couldn't stop laughing.

But I won't go, I said. I'm a pacifist.

You, a pacifist?

You know I am.

Since when?

Since always.

Since you got number nineteen.

Bullshit.

So you're going to go C.O.?

I am a C.O. I always have been a conscientious objector.

To what?

To war. All wars.

Hey, that's convenient, Gookus said.

I tucked her in and turned off the light. She shut her eyes. Leave me be now, she said. Let me rest.

All right.

You must go now.

I will.

Walter?

Yes, Mother.

I'm in so much pain.

Can I get you anything?

Spill the bottle of sleeping pills onto the bed. Fill a glass of water for me and place it on the bed stand.

You know I can't do that.

Why not?

I'm afraid.

Of what?

Doing harm.

Still whispering, with her eyes still shut, she said, You mustn't be. Pour the bottle of sleeping pills onto the blanket, or I'll take these two pillows—

Go ahead.

You'll watch?

Yes.

You won't stop me?

No.

Then why don't you assist me?

I won't help you die.

But I need an accomplice.

Do it yourself.

I'll do it.

Go ahead.

I can't. I want you to do it for me.

No.

You're cruel.

I'm sorry.

You're afraid.

Yes.

Please, Walter.

No.

A fat man with a beard and a baseball cap opened the door, slapped my hands, grabbed my thumb, and said, Hey, like, look, man, enter because my time is yours. He sat down on the floor and crossed his legs. In front of him were matches, an ashtray, nickel bags and papers, sunflower seeds, a six-pack of beer. The electricity didn't work and the phone jack was pulled out of the wall. Broken windows were boarded up or crossed with duct tape. Psychedelic posters depicting various sexual positions and states of consciousness were tacked to the walls, and from the back of the room came the sound of Indian music.

This is the draft information office, isn't it?

Was.

What do you mean?

We shut down years ago. You're the first person to come by in ages. Without the draft, no one needs guidance anymore. There's nothing to worry about, man.

He tapped his fingers on the floor and sang to accompany the music on the stereo.

I stood over him and said, Listen: listen to me: I still want to be a conscientious objector.

What for? They'll never reinstate the draft. You're in no danger of being called up.

I realize I probably won't be, but—

Probably won't be? Bullshit, man. You're in absolutely no danger. Look, I've been through the whole thing a thousand times. I was a C.O. until they found out I pulled a gun once on my girlfriend, so I put on weight until I was over the Army's limit. I know the tricks, man.

Will you at least tell me how I can apply for C.O. status?

I forget. Call the Army; they'll tell you good. You sound pretty scared, though. If they spot a coward, you can forget about C.O.

I came here for help, but you've only—

Hey, look, what am I supposed to do? I told you the

truth, didn't I? We're out of business. No more drafts. No more resisters. Nothing to worry about. I'm trying to tell you, man.

Each week all of us in Contemporary Events class were told to stand, read the article we had clipped from the newspaper, and speak up: speak up because the class was first thing in the morning and a few people in the back had the audacity to sleep. Bad boys searched for crumpled articles in pants pockets; good girls opened three-ringed binders to stories preserved between pieces of plastic. Boys read about the fire and the flood; girls read about the rescue. Some of the students could barely read and resorted to summary. Others whose families didn't subscribe to a newspaper rummaged before class for stray pages in the gutter. Those who forgot were punished after school.

At breakfast I read a story about a thirteen-year-old girl who was so trusting, so naive, so foolish that she not only jumped off her bicycle and accepted the candy but got in the car. She was stripped, and what in newspaper accounts is called abused, then she was killed. She was found in a body bag in the dark morning drizzle. Her body was badly mangled; she could be identified only by the registration number on her bicycle. The girl's mother was quoted as saying that the murderer, when caught, should not be hung until he'd first been castrated. The girl was the same age as I was. She died only a few miles from where I lived. I knew the area, the park in which her body had been trashed.

I cut out the article and the adjoining photographs—the weeping mother, the body bag in the rain—and brought them to class. I passed around the pictures while reading aloud the story. One girl said her friend knew the sister of the best friend of the dead girl, and asked me to stop reading, but the teacher said, No, please continue: maybe the girl's death would serve as an example to the rest of us to go straight home after school.

Every Tuesday night for the next five weeks the killer found an errant girl, and every Wednesday morning I read an account of the evening's events to the class. He chose different suburbs and hair colors, but always beautiful twelve- or thirteen-year-old girls whom he dressed in blue jeans and long-sleeved, white, button-down shirts, always the bruised body sealed within the plastic body bag. He left notes, written in red and misspelled, and a composite sketch of his face was drawn and circulated, although no one had actually seen him. Mothers picked up their children immediately after school and didn't allow them outside until the next morning. Detectives patrolled the streets.

Week after week I explained what had happened the night before, showed them pictures and maps. I was only thirteen years old, but for some reason I said: Don't cry. Although it was meant as encouragement to be brave, it was the wrong thing to say and they let me know they didn't like it. The teacher told me not to bring in any more articles about this series of tragic deaths. The class no longer wanted to hear about it. At recess, during lunch, and after school, gangs of girls ran up to me and said my father was probably the killer.

The next Tuesday night an anonymous voice intimated over the telephone that if another girl died that night I would be flushed down the toilet. Paint and rotten eggs spattered the front steps. I stopped answering the doorbell. I lay in bed, hoping I'd die in my sleep, since I knew another girl would be found in the morning. Teri Schraeder, who the day before during recess had told me that after what I had done she took back the one dance she had begrudgingly given me at the Christmas party, was the seventh victim—

buried in a body bag, wearing blue jeans and a white, long-sleeved, button-down shirt. When I got to school, half of the eighth grade appeared to be waiting for me. The teacher of the Contemporary Events class was holding them back with her arms out, and when I opened the entrance gate she sang out, Everybody ready? They came forward with jump ropes and bike locks for whips and white chains, and I went to my knees.

What would you do if I were raped?

What a ghastly question! What do you think I'd do?

I don't know. That's why I asked.

Don't worry about it. You'll never be raped.

Why not? What are you talking about?

You're not sexy enough. You always wear pants, never wash your hair.

You want me to dress up to get raped, Nina said.

I didn't say that.

It so happens that someone followed me home from work tonight, waited until there were no more street lamps, then made a lunge for me when I stopped to put on my mittens.

Jesus, I said and hugged her, stroked her hair. Are you okay?

Yes. I hit him in the face with my mittens and he ran away. If he had raped me, would you have shot him?

If I were with you, I would wrestle him off you, but, no, I doubt I'd shoot him.

Why must you always be so rational?

I'm sorry.

What if he had touched a knife to my throat and said, Fight me or I'll rape her?

You have such a melodramatic imagination.

What would you have done?

I don't know, I honestly—

You must not care very much about me.
I hope I'd—
Hope? My God, Walter. Hope isn't good enough.

I imagine walking up marble steps and pulling open double doors. At the other end of the room the six members of the jury sit in military uniforms at a long table. Each officer has his own microphone, and the officer at the head of the table taps his gavel and tells me to sit down. I don't have a microphone, so they can't hear my responses, but when I speak up they tell me not to shout. I read a prepared statement, five typed pages of self-righteous rebellion, and introduce scraps of evidence on my behalf: articles I've written for my high school newspaper, letters to LBJ, polemical essays, membership cards to subversive organizations. After each man has asked me a series of questions, the head officer walks to where I'm sitting and tells me to stand. He cocks his fists. I raise my arms and he says, Siddown, 1-A. . . . The Army doctor closes the door and tells me to jump up on the metal table. He quickly conducts the examination: tests my hearing, my sight, tells me to say Aah, pinches my neck, thumps my chest, feels my heart, takes my pulse, taps my knees, scrapes the bottom of my feet, then tells me to step out of my underwear. I do and try to get a hard-on. Yes, I say, I'm homosexual. He tilts his head, raises his eyebrows, puts down his clipboard, and squeezes my cock until it goes limp.

In order to evade the draft, my second cousin transferred schools every semester and told almost no one his address. He pushed dope and made blue movies. When he was drafted, he took a jar of peanut butter with him to the physical and smeared it over his ass. The doctor told him to strip, so he plopped a mound of peanut butter into his mouth and ate it. He licked his lips. The doctor ran his fingers over the smeared crease in his underwear, asked him if he often ate his own shit, and he nodded enthusiastically.

All it comes down to, Walter, with this C.O. business is that you don't want to die.

That's not true.

It's nothing to be ashamed of. No one wants to die.

That's not all there is to it.

You're scared. We're all scared.

I'm not a coward. It takes courage to do what I'm doing.

As a child you would wake up in the middle of the night and sit, crying, at the landing of the stairs until I came to comfort you.

Mother, please.

You would say that you didn't want the rest of the world to exist if you were dead. You wanted me to make sure you were preserved in ice when you died so that you could be brought back to life when a cure was discovered.

Childish fantasies.

Of course, but don't deny them. You're still afraid.

No I'm not.

Of course you are. But there's nothing to be afraid of.

You're not afraid?

I want to get it over with. Spill the pills onto the blanket, Walt, and pour me some water.

Stop it. We've been through all this before.

I spent the summer between my sophomore and junior years of high school licking envelopes for a Congressional candidate who said he wouldn't return from Washington until the war was over. At the time I believed in such statements. I sat at phone banks, calling every registered voter in the precinct, but very few of them answered and those who did were either opposed or virtually deaf. I carried a table, a chair, and voter registration cards into the wealthiest neighborhood in the state, an old woman invited me in for tea, and when I returned the table was gone. I wrote the candidate's speeches for him; halfway through every speech, he stopped, discarded the script, and spoke, he said, from the gut. He was obese. His gut was repulsive. At the dinners, no one drank enough to get drunk. At the fund-raisers, no one contributed. Our billboards were derivative. The newspaper and television advertisements were antediluvian. The campaign slogan was NO HOKUM—VOTE FOR SLOCUM. Election day I drove crippled people to the polling booth, and on the way home most of them told me they voted for the challenger. Slocum's wife was beautiful, so a week before the election a rumor was leaked that his opponent had spent campaign funds in downtown massage parlors, and Slocum won in a landslide. I started that rumor.

I write a letter to appeal the jury's decision. I write: *I must refuse to play any part in the military. I would have to kill myself rather than cause the death of another man. Even if I were not required to use a weapon, I would be unable to serve the army in any capacity. I value nothing more than my own conscience. As a child I did not play with guns. I would not have fought in the American Revolution or the Second World War. My parents taught me always to be good, never to do bad. I am a highly moral human being. I am prepared to accept the consequences of my actions.*

As a wide receiver, I would run intricate patterns, then stand all alone in the middle of the field, waving my hands, calling for the ball. I never dropped a pass, but when I was hit hard, I would typically tighten up and fumble. I was the best softball player in the neighborhood, but as we grew older, we began to play overhand, fast-pitch hardball, and I started flinching. Trying to beat out a ground ball, I would always slow down so that the throw to first base would arrive ahead of me and I would avoid getting hit in the head with a wild toss. Batting, I was afraid of getting hit with the pitch; fielding, I dreaded bad hops off the rocky infield. No one could shoot a basketball as well as I could, but I was afraid to drive into the complicated middle of the key, where I would get banged up, and everyone knew that, so they guarded me tight and shut me off. I could run a hundred yards in 10.6 seconds, but I had very long legs and the track coach insisted that I run high hurdles; I stutter-stepped before each hurdle to make sure I cleared it, and came in last. I feared the black rubber mats, the sudden loss of balance, the pressure on the skull, the slap of feet and legs to the ground: I flunked gym because I couldn't turn somersaults. Having never learned to dive, I jumped in the pool feet first. The swimming instructor dragged me to the edge of the diving board, positioned my arms and legs, held me in the air for a second, then dropped me into the pool. At the last instant I turned my face, and water broke my fall like a bed of electric needles. What was I scared of? Why was I so afraid of getting hurt? I was under the mistaken impression there was such a thing as a clean sprint through the night without spikes or hurdles.

Did you kill anybody in World War II?
Might have. Don't know. Can't tell. Hard to say.

Why don't you know?

You're all firing your weapons at once, so you don't know if your bullet killed the dead man or the bullet of the man next to you killed him.

But do you think you did?

Perhaps.

Perhaps?

Well, yes, I did. Why, what's the matter, son?

Why did you have to kill him?

Who?

The man you killed, perhaps.

Hey, stop looking at me with those wide eyes of yours. He was shooting at me. What was I supposed to have done?

Were you scared?

No.

But he was shooting at you?

It's okay. It's okay. He missed.

My father killed Hitler. He was with a squad of soldiers, one of whom would have killed Hitler if Hitler had not killed himself first. He was part of a squad that surrounded the bunker in which Hitler killed himself. He was in another part of Germany when Hitler killed himself. He was in Okinawa at the time. He was in Brooklyn and read about it in his newspaper. He couldn't afford to subscribe to a newspaper and read about it in someone else's newspaper. He couldn't read English and someone had to explain to him what had happened.

My father said he volunteered to serve in the Army in World War II. He said he was drafted at about the same time he volunteered. He didn't remember which was first. He said he was drafted just days before he would have volunteered.

My father put his arm around my shoulder, took off his glasses, then half whispered into my ear that he was drafted but failed the physical examination due to a problem with his left leg and returned home.

What sort of problem? I asked. In eighteen years I'd never heard or seen that he had any problem with his left leg.

It's healed since then, he said, shaking his head and gesturing toward a vague point in the past to indicate that I needn't and wouldn't know more.

I imagine showing the new letter from the draft board to my father, who says: What does this stand for—Cowards Only? He dances around me, tousling my hair, tugging my ears, pinching my nose, and stinging my face with rapid, openhanded blows to back me into a corner. He pins my arms, pokes me in the stomach, knees me in the groin. I turn toward the wall, with my head in my hands, but when he clutches my throat, I swing around to face him, throwing my arms up and outward. I hit him, hard, across the jaw.

I didn't mean it, I say. I'm sorry—I didn't hurt you, did I?

He falls to the floor, overacting a bit, I'm certain, but clearly stunned.

My new dream goes like this: in the middle of the desert my father offers me water from his canteen, which I accept with outstretched hands and drink until I'm no longer thirsty. He takes off his boots and shakes out pebbles, dirt, dead leaves. Lizards crawl around, looking for shade under rocks and short shrubs. When he untwists the black top of the canteen he finds nothing but the inside of the container.

You drank all the water, he says.

Yes, I say, I was thirsty.

That's all we had left. We won't be able to survive.

I'm sorry. I didn't know.

Of course you knew.

I'm sorry.

We may die, Walter.

We won't die.

We may. You have no concern for anyone other than—

There's a cactus plant out there.

Where?

Out there, out in the distance.

I can't see it.

Your eyes are bad.

I don't see it.

He unties the knots in his backpack and removes his eyeglasses. He rubs the lenses with his shirt until they're filthy, then gazes into the distance, contemplating the sheer magnitude of this inhuman habitat. A quarter mile away, due west, partially hidden among rock piles and dying trees, stands a giant cactus plant.

I'll race you for the water in the cactus, I say.

I shouldn't run. My leg's bothering me.

Then the water's mine.

I make a false start, but he shouts at me to wait.

Really, Walt, my bad leg's bothering me.

He unstraps the canteen from his belt, takes the backpack off his shoulders, and gives both the canteen and the backpack to me. He stretches his legs by touching his toes and doing deep knee bends. He builds up sand to serve as a starting block and crouches down in a sprinter's ready position, dusting dirt and sand off his fingers onto his pants leg, bending his left leg forward, shooting his right leg back, and balancing himself on the balls of his feet and his fingertips. With his feet buried in the sand, his shoulders hunched over and shaking, and his head pointed straight ahead as if he's a bird dog, he rocks until he's set. He's serious.

I fasten the canteen to my belt and pull the straps of the backpack over my shoulders. Although I feel weighted down, I pull one knee and then the other up to my chest, stretching. I'm thirsty; I definitely want to win. I look out across the dry desert and toward the cactus in the distance, then back to him. He's poised, ready to run. A quarter of a mile is only once around the track, I say to myself, and bend down a little and put my hands on my knees.

Who's going to start us? I ask.

I will. Runners, take your mark, he says and shakes one leg and then the other behind him. He crouches down low and spits into the dirt.

Are you sure your leg is all right?

Get set.

I'd hate for you to hurt it or make it any worse.

Go, he says. He gets off to such a good start that I think maybe he's jumped the gun. I chase after him, calling out that in order to be absolutely fair to both parties involved we should at least think about starting over again, but he ignores me and clenches his fists, lengthens his stride, and kicks up pebbles as he increases his lead. Although he's only a few yards ahead, I can't close the gap because the backpack bounces up and down on my shoulders and weighs a ton and the canteen knocks against my thighs and stomach, slowing me down further. My chest fills with dry air.

Bounding over the desert, avoiding rocks and brush, we approach the cactus plant, which is huge: four stems curve up from the base and one major stem sticks straight up into the air thirty feet like a thick green finger. In the distance, to both sides of us, north and south, are rocks worn away into jagged, meaningless shapes. The sky is clear light blue, completely open and empty except for a flock of sand grouse flying overhead, looking for water.

We near the cactus and I can hear him gasping for breath when I edge up on him. He's trying to hold on, but I can tell he isn't going to make it. He has nothing left: his bad leg is wobbly, his head is bobbing up and down, his neck muscles are straining. He's tight, and I'm a step behind. I let my arms swing more freely and bring my knees up higher, all the way to my chest, as I catch a second wind and sprint by him, shouting, racing for the cactus, forgetting about the backpack and canteen, finally hitting my stride with my arms and legs working together smoothly and powerfully.

He falls. His knees buckle. He loses the lead as well as his balance and tumbles into the dirt, headfirst, arms stretched out flat to break his fall. He scrapes his hands across ragged rocks, skidding across the desert on his stomach. The sand grouse sweep down to see what's happened; I don't stop running until I reach the cactus. I trample over the shrubs and sharp brush surrounding the cactus, take my knife out of my pocket, and cut through the clustered spines of the lowest stem, the only one I'm able to reach. It's coated with wax. I prick myself on the bristles and my fingers bleed. The cut stems drip water, which I cup in my hands.

He's holding his hip and still breathing hard. His hands are cut and bloody, and his right leg is shaking slightly. His tongue sticks out of his open mouth. I kneel down and offer him the water, but he turns on his side, onto his bad leg, away from me.

I had you, he says. Goddamnit, I had you. You're slow, Walter. I had you.

I raise my hands to my face to drink.

Innocence

It was a tight squeeze, even for a kid—this narrow little lav that had nails sticking out of the wall, and above him a silver shower nozzle that dripped slowly, like water torture. The cloth curtain, pushed back, was ripped. A hissing sound came from the toilet, and although Walt kept jiggling the handle, it wouldn't stop. He kicked off his shoes and, standing on the bench, hung up his pants, underwear, and shirt on one of the hooks. Naked, he shivered. After taking a towel off a nail and climbing down off the bench, Walt squirmed into his damp swimming trunks, which were blue with a weird contraption in the center of the crotch: thick white string that crisscrossed and had to be laced up like boots. He had some trouble, but he knotted it at the top, let the drawstring fall into his trunks, and folded over the flap so the braided network didn't show in front. He was seven years old and weighed forty-six pounds.

Walt got back up on the bench and stood on his tiptoes, pushing open the window and looking toward the beach. It was cold out; there weren't many people scattered along the beach and almost no one was in the water. The ocean extended for as far as he could see in either direction, and he thought the horizon was the other side of the world. The water looked dark, murky. Men in black skin-diving suits surfaced and splashed their way onto the beach.

"Is anything the matter, Walt?"

"No."

"Have you locked yourself in?"

"No."

His mother tried the door and said it was locked.

"I'm coming," he said.

"Let's all go get in the water before the tide starts coming in."

"Coming."

Walt climbed down off the bench, wrapped the towel around his neck, tugged on his trunks until he was certain they wouldn't slide down his legs at exactly the wrong moment, unlocked the door, and pushed it open. His mother came out of the kitchen, carrying a picnic basket full of food for lunch. His father held a hardcover book called *The Judgment of Julius and Ethel Rosenberg* in one hand and towels and blankets in the other. Ellen, wearing a one-piece bathing suit, carried an inner tube at her side and told him to stop dawdling.

"Lend me a hand, Walt," his mother said.

Helpful and altruistic as ever, Walt plucked the plastic thermos from the picnic basket and scooted out the house ahead of his family, which had spent a good portion of the morning waiting for him to get ready. The three of them walked together, behind him, down to the beach. Low clouds still blocked the sun and made the morning dark and foggy and bleak. No soft shimmer of rays on water; Walt didn't want to go in. Nobody else was swimming.

Walt's mother chased after Ellen, calling out to her about the tide coming in soon, as she bounced the inner tube toward the water. After lying face down on the blanket and poking his sunglasses onto the bridge of his nose, Walt's father opened up his book and began again telling Walt about how, as Julius entered the brightly lit, white-walled execution chamber, he winced involuntarily; how, as he approached the oak-paneled electric chair, his knees buckled; how Ethel spurned the efforts of guards to strap her hands and secure the electrodes to her head and leg, then needed two more shocks when her brave heart was still beating after the standard three.

What was the point of these gruesome details? Walt didn't know and didn't especially care. He just wanted to get away from this weird world of his father's and ran over the cool, sparkling sand to the edge of the ocean, where his sister and mother were wading in the shallow water. Ellen stood up with the tire around the bottom of her legs, bobbing slightly in the water. A few yards deeper out, Walt's mother dipped her face into the icy water and splashed her chest and arms. Red seaweed floated by on the surface. Walt's feet slipped on jagged rocks. He stood at the fringe of the ocean and let trickles at the tail end of waves slap up against his legs. His mother frog-kicked even farther out. Ellen moved over toward her and clambered up on the inner tube, paddling, as it carried her out to sea.

Walt cupped his hands over his mouth and called: "Carry me in the water, Mommy."

"No. You've swum in pools. This is no different. You can do it."

"I can't."

"Try," Ellen suggested. "Don't be such a baby. It's only water. You won't drown."

"Yes, Walt. First put your head in the water to get acclimated. Then blow a few bubbles, like you know how to do. Kick—"

"I'm afraid."

"You needn't be, honey."

"Yeah, don't be such a baby, Walt."

"Give me the tire," he said.

"No, it's mine."

"Let me use it."

"Swim out and take it from me."

"Let Walt use it," his mother said, then swam back to Ellen and hoisted her up out of the inner tube. Ellen flipped over on her back and floated easily. The inner tube drifted away, but Walt's mother caught up with it and pushed it ahead of herself with her elbows as she swam toward him with swift strokes. She dove underwater, gathered him up in her arms, and put him atop the inner tube.

"No, don't," Walt said as she dragged him out toward deeper water.

He was so small that he would have fallen through if he'd sat in the middle. He squirmed around, trying to get a foothold, clutching onto the wet rubber, holding on for what he thought might be his life. From the beach, Ellen laughed and waved both hands in the air.

Walt gripped the sides of her inner tube and looked down at his mother, who was treading water and seemed tired. He looked back at the beach and couldn't find his father anywhere in the distance, although Walt knew he was always either sleeping or thinking about the Rosenbergs—how, for instance, he had stood with thousands of other people somewhere in New York City, holding a sign saying WE ARE IN-

NOCENT and weeping openly when a man named Howard Fast announced that the Rosenbergs were dead. Walt knew that, when his father coached tennis at a summer resort in the Catskills in the 1930s, he had become acquainted with the couple who later adopted the Rosenberg children. Was that why his father remained so fascinated with the case?

There was still no sun and the water felt quite cold when it splashed into Walt's lap. His mother continued tugging around the old tire; her head bobbing up and down, in and out of the water.

"Jump off, Walt," she said. "I'll catch you."

"You won't."

"I will. I promise."

"I'll drown."

"Don't be silly. Nothing can happen. Swim into my hands, sweetheart."

"Let's go back."

"Come on now. You can do it. Your father and sister are watching."

"Daddy's not watching."

"He is."

There he was at the shoreline, pumping the air with the book in his hand.

"Don't be afraid. It's warm, and there aren't any fish or seaweed out here. It's pure ocean; it's for swimming. Come on, Walt. Be a man."

"Let's go back."

"No turning back now."

Like a dolphin, she leapt out of the water and gripped the inner tube. She stopped for a moment to catch her breath, and while Walt tried to wriggle away on the edge of the squeaking rubber, she tilted the tube toward her so that it was standing rather than floating on the surface of the sea. Through the center of the tire he went flying backward into the Pacific, which immediately sucked him under. He kicked his feet and shook his arms, but he forgot to close his mouth and nearly gagged on a gallon of water. His mother seemed to keep backing away from him a bit with each stroke he swam toward her, so that, in spite of the fact that his ears were stopped up and he couldn't hear a sound, and that the chilly water had made his arms and legs tingle and then clench up tight, and that, compared to the Rosenbergs (Ethel, in particular), he felt like such a coward, he was swimming in open water.

A NOTE ON THE TYPE

The text of this book was set in
Electra, a typeface designed by
W. A. Dwiggins (1880–1956). This
face cannot be classified as either
modern or old style. It is not based on
any historical model; nor does it echo
any particular period or style.
It avoids the extreme contrasts
between thick and thin elements
that mark most modern faces, and
attempts to give a feeling of fluidity,
power, and speed.

Composed by Creative Graphics, Inc.,
Allentown, Pennsylvania

Printed and bound by The Haddon Craftsmen,
Scranton, Pennsylvania

Typography and binding design by
Dorothy Schmiderer Baker